SERVANTS

OF THE MIST

SERVANTS OF THE MIST

GARY BREWER

Bridge Resources
Louisville, Kentucky

Grateful acknowledgment is made to Little, Brown and Company for permission to reprint excerpts from *Familiar Quotations: A Collection of Passages, Phrases and Proverbs Traced to Their Sources in Ancient and Modern Literature,* by John Bartlett, copyright © 1968 Little, Brown and Company.

Edited by David M. Dobson

Book interior and cover design by Robert McAtee

Cover illustration by Marjie Fall

First edition

Published by Bridge Resources

Louisville, Kentucky

Web site address: http://www.bridgeresources.org

PRINTED IN THE UNITED STATES OF AMERICA

98 99 00 01 02 03 04 05 06 07 — 10 9 8 7 6 5 4 3 2 1

Library of Congress Cataloging-in-Publication Data

Brewer, Gary, date.
    Servants of the Mist / Gary Brewer. — 1st ed.
       p.   cm.
    Summary: Thirteen-year-old Gurion feels drawn to a mysterious
island where, through a series of fantastical experiences, he comes
to understand his purpose in life.
    ISBN 1-57895-058-9
    [1. Conduct of life—Fiction.]   I. Title.
    PZ7.B7569Sg 1998
    [Fic]—dc21i   98-16357
                                                     AC

This book is dedicated to the generation of hope who will lead us into the promised land of the new millennium.

To know how to live is all my calling and all my art.

-Michel de Montaigne (1533-1592)

1
THE CALLING

A lone canoe slipped almost unnoticed through the sticky morning mist that hung like the web of some immense spider over the silent lake. In the canoe a boy, small for his fourteen years, paddled awkwardly—slapping the water frantically as if trying to escape the clutches of whatever it was that waited unseen in the gray fog.

"Beware!" the voice had warned him, now weeks ago. "The lake is filled with the waters of fear."

Remembering the voice that had sent him, Gurion felt again the calm resolve that was the gift of the voice. He began to paddle with longer, more determined strokes.

The island, he thought. Not much farther. The end—no, the beginning of my journey.

The predawn grayness began to be transformed by the haunting pastels of the coming sunrise. The gray cloud that clung to the waters of the lake turned a bloody red. Gurion held tightly to the paddle. "Relax," he told himself. "It's just a lake like any other lake." But even before the words had formed in his mind, he knew they were not true.

This was a lake like no other. It had taken him days to summon up the courage to attempt to cross it. Now he was more than halfway to the island. He could see its gnarled trees burdened with moss. He could see the heavy mist creeping between the trees. What was he getting himself into?

He had been chosen for a purpose he did not yet understand. But why? Of all the people in the world, why had *he* been singled out? Was it only his imagination? Was he losing his mind?

No, the authority of the voice was unmistakable, irresistible. Responding to it, answering its call, sitting in this particular canoe in the chill of the morning's mist—here and now—Gurion had never been more certain about anything in his life.

The lake was the subject of a variety of legends. It occupied the crater of what had been a magnificent mountain. Hundreds, perhaps thousands of years ago, a volcanic explosion had blown the top half of the mountain into the atmosphere—millions of tons of solid rock turned instantly into a powdery dust that the winds carried away. The crater had filled with the rain and snow of countless winters, and from the depths of the once-great mountain, magma had bubbled to the surface, cooled, and formed an island.

No one knew how deep the waters were. No one knew what caused the mists that crawled across the lake morning and night in every season of the year.

The island, belched up from the fiery underworld, supported an odd variety of flora and fauna. The trees and shrubs were bent and gnarled. Every imaginable species of thorny plant seemed to be represented. And though the island was uninhabited—perhaps uninhabitable—by human beings, strange stories of bizarre life forms circulated among the people who, like Gurion, lived in areas surrounding the lake. Several eyewitnesses even claimed to have seen giant lizardlike creatures with scaled wings.

Gurion had heard the stories. He had always been cautioned to stay away from the island. He thought now how compelling the voice must be to have allowed him to overcome all those warnings and fears.

The island was getting closer. Another five minutes or so of paddling and he would be there. Gurion strained his eyes, trying to see through the mist that drifted everywhere.

If only the dreadful fog were not so thick, Gurion thought.

Then, in the predawn light that filtered through the mist, he saw movement on the land ahead. It appeared to be a human figure dressed in dark clothing, bent and gnarled like the trees.

A sudden clearing in the mist brought the approaching beach into view. It was rocky, but not impassable. A crooked finger of land jutted out into the water as if it were trying to grab hold of Gurion's canoe. Gurion took advantage of the clearing and landed his canoe on the narrow peninsula. The instant he set foot on the island he could see the first rays of the sunrise. Then, just as quickly, the sun disappeared behind the encroaching mist.

Gurion walked carefully down the peninsula toward the main part of the island. A well-worn path made the going much easier than he had anticipated. What kind of animals had made this path? he wondered. As he approached the body of the island he saw that the path led around the exterior for a way and then cut in toward the middle.

Gurion stopped and peered cautiously through the mist that covered the path. A thick underbrush obscured any view he might have had to the sides. The trees that grew through the tangled shrubs seemed to be holding distorted poses in some eerie primeval dance.

The light of morning now warmed the land and gave Gurion the courage to continue toward the heart of the island. An inner voice called him deeper and deeper into the interior.

By midmorning he found himself in a clearing that had some unmistakably human touches. A circle of stones marked off a large arena that had been filled with a mixture of sand and sawdust. A hand-hewn bench invited him to be seated. Gurion sat down nervously and took inventory of his situation.

The first thing he realized was that this bench was somehow "home." He knew he was precisely where he should be at this particular instant in time. Still, he was a three-hour walk from his canoe. And that made him a bit uncomfortable because he was not at all sure he wanted to spend the night here alone.

He was weary from the canoe trip and from his walk on the island. Part of him wanted to stretch out on the bench and sleep. He was hungry. He had not eaten since early this morning—just before he climbed into the canoe. He had no sense of how long he was supposed to wait, or just what it was he was waiting for. He decided to eat part of the lunch in his backpack.

Two hard-boiled eggs and half a peanut butter sandwich later, Gurion was still waiting for something to happen. He resisted the urge to sleep because he wanted to be prepared to confront, face-to-face, whoever or whatever the voice had sent him to meet.

The sun was directly overhead and the fog beginning to burn off when Gurion first felt the presence of another being. He wanted to scream and run but didn't know which way to go. He felt the hair stand up on the back of his neck.

A dark cloud covered the sun and sent a shadow crawling across the arena. Gurion jumped up and turned a slow full circle. He saw nothing. He backed away from the bench and was about to bolt down the path toward his canoe when his feet became tangled in the thorny underbrush.

"What are you doing on my island?"

The strange voice startled Gurion. They were the first words he had heard in hours. The voice sounded out of place in this wild place.

"Who are you, and what are you doing on my island?"

Gurion turned to face his challenger.

Out of the underbrush crawled a large spidery figure. A black-hooded tunic that bore the symbol of a red hourglass was tied at the waist over a tight-fitting rubbery suit. The shiny black material seemed impenetrable and slipped through the thorns unscratched. Gloves and boots protected long crooked appendages.

Gurion could find no words. He tugged at the rope of thorns, but his legs were caught. It was impossible to run away.

His heart pounded. He stared at the shiny black figure as it approached him through the web of thorns. Then the world began to spin. He felt himself in a vortex of fear, whirling out of control. He was falling—falling through the mist.

When Gurion awoke he was lying on a bed of straw. An old woman was sitting on the ground next to him, holding his hand. Her eyes were closed, and she was humming softly. Whatever it was she sang, it seemed to have a calming effect on Gurion, for he no longer felt frightened.

He glanced around at his surroundings, wondering how long he had been unconscious. It appeared that he was in a large cave. Torches lit the room dimly, and he could see rocky walls of black stone. Who had brought him to this cave? Would he be able to find his way back to the canoe? Was he a prisoner or a guest? He felt strangely secure—as if he were in no immediate danger. The old woman appeared to be asleep. Gurion slowly slid his hand from hers and sat up. She opened her eyes.

"I didn't mean to wake you," Gurion said.

She looked into his eyes. "You were sent here by the voice."

"Do you know why?" Gurion asked weakly, looking away.

"I know that you are Gurion, the lion, one of the chosen."

Gurion wondered how this woman knew his name and the animal he had been named for. He wondered what it all meant.

He had known he felt chosen for something ever since he first heard the voice. He also knew he was willing to serve the voice. Just the fact that he was here on this island, alone, was evidence of that.

"Are you the person I was sent to meet?"

The old woman laughed gently. "Yes, I am Kendra, but I must be far different from what you were expecting to have startled you so."

Puzzled, Gurion tried to unravel what the old woman was saying. When had she startled him? Certainly not here in the cave. The only thing that had startled him was the shiny black figure that had trapped him in the thorny underbrush. Was it possible that she was the spidery creature that had thrown him into such a panic?

"You carried me here through the brush?"

"Yes."

"I thought you were some kind of strange—I guess I've

heard too many stories about this island."

Kendra smiled. "There's nothing wrong with a healthy imagination. Besides, the stories are not without foundation. There is much here that defies rational explanation. When I found you in the brush you were unconscious. Your leg was tangled in the thorns. As I was freeing your leg you awakened briefly, screamed, and again lost consciousness. I carried you here so that you would be safe."

Gurion's head was swimming, trying to remember. "Then it was not you who spoke to me?"

"I'm afraid I never had a chance. At least not until now."

"Something was watching me as I approached the island in my canoe. I think it followed me to the arena and spied on me as I waited. Something like a giant spider."

"How long were you at the arena?" she asked.

"A couple of hours, I think—from midmorning to about noon."

"And you sat on the bench while you waited?"

"Yes."

The old woman had gotten to her feet and was pacing the floor, thinking. "It could mean something, or it could be nothing at all. The bench, perhaps the whole island, is enchanted. Most of what takes place here is illusion."

"The spider was no illusion." Gurion spoke softly, almost as if he were trying to convince himself.

A rumble from the depths of the earth brought Gurion to his feet. Kendra moved quickly to put on a wool shawl and then took one of the torches from the wall of the cave. "If you feel able to walk we can make the twilight gate. We have fifteen minutes. Otherwise there is no gate until sunrise."

Gurion wanted to ask what gate she was talking about but she was already halfway across the cave, getting a torch for him. It was obvious that there was little time to waste.

A narrow tunnel led them deeper and deeper under the island. It appeared to Gurion that the tunnel was the result of a giant air pocket trapped in the magma before it had cooled and hardened into rock. The sides and top of the tunnel were smooth and shiny. The path itself was slick in places, but the old woman moved quickly, as if she had traveled the route a hundred times.

The path leveled out and opened into an enormous room deep in the earth. Some kind of electrical lighting had been devised, and Gurion could see that the ceiling of the cave was fifty or sixty feet above the path. Water leaked from above and ran down the walls.

"Be very careful here to stay on the path," Kendra warned. "Our way leads us out onto a precipice over a bottomless pit. The edges of the path are lit with safety lights."   .

Gurion could see the path outlined for perhaps a hundred yards like a narrow runway, but then the lights ended. "What is at the end of the lights?" he asked. But she was already too far in front of him to hear. Gurion hesitated, and his world began to spin.

"Hurry! We have only a minute or two to reach the twilight gate." Kendra was already at the end of the runway. She shouted her command with such urgency that Gurion was snapped out of his dizziness. He swallowed hard and then made his way carefully down the lighted path. At the end of the path a wooden drawbridge crossed the expanse of nothingness that separated them from the lights on the other side of the great room.

"This is the gate that leads into the Hall of Service. It is the only way in or out. The drawbridge is activated by the first rays of sunrise and the last rays of sunset. It is on a fifteen-minute timer."

The bridge itself was perhaps fifty feet long. At its end another lighted runway led precariously to the main path on the other side of what looked to be a great room. Before they had reached the main path, the earth began to groan and rumble again and the bridge lifted slowly until it stood like a tower at the end of the narrow ledge.

"We have only a few minutes until the lights of the great room are extinguished. Then we will have to rely on our torches. It is about a thirty-minute walk to the Hall."

The great room, like the network of tunnels leading to and from it, appeared to be the result of gases that had bubbled up into the molten lava when the island and the lake bed were being formed. The volcano had for hundreds of years remained dormant. And yet it seemed to Gurion that the volcano must somehow be responsible for the morning and evening mists. The water that seeped from the ceiling and ran down the walls had to go somewhere. The air above the bottomless pit had felt warm and moist. Perhaps it found its way to the surface and condensed when it combined with the cool night air.

The tunnel that led from the great room was, for the most part, easily passable. Only occasionally did it narrow enough to make it necessary to crawl on hands and knees. A steady draft of cool fresh air was both refreshing and reassuring.

Kendra made her way quickly and gracefully through the system of passages, and Gurion had to hurry to keep up with her. At last the path widened and the tunnel expanded into a smaller room that was lighted in a manner similar to the great room.

"This is the anteroom to the Hall of Service," Kendra explained. "We must wait here until we are summoned."

Gurion looked around. The walls were smooth and shiny as if glazed in a potter's kiln. The path appeared to end in this cavern. There was no visual evidence of any way out of the anteroom except by the tunnel that led back to where they'd come.

Benches had been cut out of the stone on one wall. On another wall, opposite the entry tunnel, letters had been carved in an arch over the blank stone. The letters read MINISTRARE EST VIVERE. It seemed to be some sort of name or motto.

Kendra had disposed of the torches and seated herself on one of the stone benches. She hummed softly, the same tune that Gurion had heard when he woke up in the cave. Her face reflected a calm and patient wisdom.

"How long will we have to wait?" Gurion asked her hesitantly.

"Time has little meaning inside the Hall. But our

presence and our need will be felt. You have been called to be a servant of the mist, and you have answered the call. That which has chosen you will know of your arrival. When you have made yourself ready, you will be admitted."

The old woman's voice was little more than a whisper. She seemed to be speaking out of a state of complete relaxation. Gurion noticed that her breathing was deep and steady, her eyes unfocused.

There were so many questions he wanted to ask, but he sensed the answers were to be found within the Hall of Service. He did not doubt the existence of the Hall, even though he saw no possible entrances. Too much had happened on this island already for him to doubt the possibility of anything.

"Will you be coming with me?"

"No. You will be initiated into service and then sent back to me. I am the gatekeeper. When you know true service, I will be here to lead you back into the world. But for now you have much to learn."

Gurion watched the old woman settle slowly onto the hard stone bench. "Then you will be my teacher?"

"Ah. Each of us has many teachers. Even this stone bench can tell you much. But ultimately each of us has only one true teacher. You must find your own way. Pursuit of the true service is a quest as compelling as the search for the Holy Grail—and just as elusive."

Kendra's meditative state pulled Gurion into a rhythm that slowed his pulse and relieved his anxiety. He took several deep breaths and thought he must be prepared for whatever would follow.

He was not quite sure he understood what the old woman meant by true service. He thought he knew what it meant to serve. And he understood that he had been called into service by the voice. He had answered the call willingly. But what did it mean to serve the voice?

He felt himself drifting into a state of deep relaxation. The stone bench on which he sat softened and then began to dissolve. He was sinking slowly into solid stone.

Strangely, he was no longer frightened, as he had been several times since his journey began. He felt calm, at peace. He sensed that this could be the way into the Hall. But he needed guidance, a push in the right direction. He turned to Kendra to ask her what to do. She was gone.

Jolted by the old woman's absence, Gurion's eyes sought her desperately. His sense of panic upset the peace he knew moments ago. He felt the stone slab hardening quickly.

No! He needed to act for himself. Kendra had said that one must find one's own way. He forced himself to relax and focused his attention on the elaborate inscription he faced: MINISTRARE EST VIVERE. He felt the stone bench slowly become soft and yielding once again.

As he concentrated on the motto, Gurion thought he saw the wall slowly lowering. Then he realized he was rising! He was hovering, in a sitting position, about one foot above the bench and was moving steadily toward the solid stone wall under the arch of letters. He sensed no motion, yet the wall was rapidly approaching. He knew he would strike it if he continued in the direction he was headed. He tried to slow himself, but he had no way to control his movement. As he and the wall were about to collide, Gurion flinched and closed his eyes. He instinctively expected to crash into solid stone, but the blow didn't come. After a moment he opened his eyes. He felt nothing, saw nothing. He might as well have left them closed. All was darkness and stillness. Seconds, perhaps hours passed. He could discern no difference.

Gurion couldn't even tell if he was awake or unconscious. Awareness faded to nonawareness. Gurion began to lose himself.

"Hold on," came the voice. "Cling to your existence. Just a little farther."

Farther to what? Gurion wanted to shout. But, as before, the voice gave him strength, and Gurion regained a sense of himself.

A sudden bright light blinded him. He couldn't see anything at all, but presently he felt the pressure of a hard, even surface underneath his feet. As he forced himself to stand perfectly still, his eyes gradually adjusted to the dazzling light of the Hall of Service.

The sight was spectacular. Every surface in the Hall was of perfect, unbroken volcanic stone, as if it had been molded directly out of the molten rock from which it came. There were no breaks, no seams. The ceiling arched up an incredible distance, shedding light down on Gurion's face. The Hall was about a hundred paces from side to side, and so long that Gurion couldn't quite make out the end of it.

On each wall there were doors, flanked by stone statues of various creatures and people—statues that seemed to rise out of the very floor itself.

Every door was different. Looking across the Hall, Gurion saw steel doors, heavy plastic doors, wooden doors, stone doors, and even doors made of huge gemstones. They were of different colors, shapes, and sizes. And every door had a number, letter, or both carved above it in the solid stone.

Gurion looked back at the wall behind him. There had been no door from the anteroom side, yet he saw a door behind him now. It was a familiar hollow core door with a modern brass-plated doorknob. The number above the door was 21N.

People of every description wandered the Hall. Knights in shining armor mixed with green, pointy-eared figures wearing shiny metallic clothing. Gurion saw shaggy-haired people, some wearing animal furs, standing next to button-down-collar business executives. Some were dressed well and others were not. People of all races and cultures—past, present, and future—were represented. It was a bewildering display.

Gurion waded into the flow, unsure of how to proceed. There didn't seem to be anyone in charge. Small groups of people moved with purpose toward obvious objectives, while others stood and conversed. Gurion was trying to decide on a plan of action when a balding man in a trim suit approached him.

"Is this your first visit to the Hall of Service?"

"Yes, it is," Gurion replied gratefully. "I seem to have been called for some purpose, but I don't understand what I'm supposed to do now that I am here."

"I know the feeling."

"Were you called here too?"

"Yes, I've made several trips to and from the Hall. And I still don't know the reason. My name is Barlow."

Gurion felt a link with this gentle soul. "I'm Gurion." He turned to look at the others. "Do you know what all these people are doing here?"

"I know they've all been called, for whatever reason, to serve the voice—just as you and I have been called. We are all initiates here. We must learn what service means before we can serve the voice in the world."

Gurion softly repeated Kendra's parting words: "A quest as compelling and elusive as the search for the Holy Grail."

"Well said, my friend." Barlow reflected. "Sounds like you have been listening to Kendra."

"You know her? Has she led all these people to the Hall?"

"Many of them, if not all. She is the gatekeeper—at least for our world, for our time."

"There seem to be people here from past ages and from future times," Gurion suggested.

"Yes. And perhaps from different worlds. I don't know."

"But how is that possible?"

"There is no time in the Hall. It is of a dimension beyond time, beyond space. There are doors to every possible time and place in our world and beyond."

"How do you know that?" Gurion asked incredulously.

"Because I've been through some of the doors. We are here in pursuit of the true service. Folks in the Hall call these excursions 'dream quests,' because after you return to the Hall they seem like dreams. I guess it is the only way our brains can handle it."

"And the dream quests teach us about service?"

Barlow paused for a moment before answering. "Well, I suppose I have learned something from my quests. But I have much more to learn. I used to think that service meant giving customers what they wanted, when they wanted, for the right price." He winked at Gurion. "Remember that, and you could climb to the top of the business world like I did."

"How do you know which door to go through?" Gurion asked.

Barlow smiled. "I'm not sure it matters a whole lot. I'm afraid some of us may have to try them all before we finally get everything figured out. And yet others learn quickly. Kendra may be taking you back before you know it."

"What about the numbers and letters over the doors? Are they some kind of code?"

"Beats me," Barlow confessed. "I suppose they have significance to someone, but I've never figured them out. I only know that the lower numbers take you back in time and the higher numbers into the future."

One of the green people with pointy ears tapped Barlow on the shoulder and whispered something in his ear. Barlow nodded and then turned back to Gurion. "I've been invited to accompany Zohar. Zohar, meet Gurion."

Zohar touched her thumbs together and bowed in recognition. "My world defines service as obedience without questions. My friend Barlow wants to see it for himself. You are welcome to join us if you like."

"Thank you," Gurion said, "but I'm still learning about the Hall." He turned to Barlow. "Good luck on your quest. And thank you for what you have shared."

Barlow and Zohar walked about a third of the way down the length of the room and left through a heavy plastic door marked 49F.

Gurion understood now why the small groups were walking purposefully toward an objective. They were headed toward particular doors. Occasionally, Gurion would see someone exit through one of the doors alone. But most people went in pairs or small groups.

Gurion started reflecting on his own ideas about service. He had never really thought much about it. What did it mean to serve? Certainly it implied obedience, but did it mean "obedience without questions," as Zohar had defined it? It seemed to him that service also implied helping someone, fighting for what was right and true. He wanted to test those ideas—but how, where?

"*Umph!*" Gurion was knocked to the floor by a burly knight, dressed entirely in a suit of heavy plate armor and bearing a giant sword strapped to his back.

"Pardon me. I didn't see thee standing there. My vision is somewhat impaired by this visor." The knight helped Gurion to his feet and attempted to dust him off with his iron-clad glove.

"Ouch!" The glove nearly knocked Gurion down again.

"There. I am Wilfred, at thy service." The knight tried to bow, but all he could manage was a slight tilt from the knees.

"My name is Gurion—the lion, so I'm told. But I'm afraid I don't know what that means. I was just standing here daydreaming, trying to think about service."

The knight responded as if he were reciting something he had memorized. "Service is defending the weak, being faithful to thy liege lord and chivalrous to the ladies. Perhaps, squire, thou desirest a demonstration. Follow me!" The knight spun around and started walking away.

Gurion was a bit bemused by this speech but decided to take the knight up on his offer. So he followed him down the crowded Hall.

The knight stopped at a heavy oaken door with a crossbeam. Above it was the number 13MC. He opened the thick door easily with one hand.

Looking through it, Gurion caught a glimpse of an evening forest. A white stallion decked out in ornamental bard was tied to a tree. Blankets were set out on the ground, along with a loaf of bread and a flask. The knight stepped right into the forest. Gurion, after a moment's hesitation, followed.

The heavy door swung shut with a bang. Gurion turned around abruptly and found himself looking into a hollow tree. There was no sign of the Hall.

Some say that the age of chivalry is past, that the spirit of romance is dead. The age of chivalry is never past, so long as there is a wrong left unredressed on earth.

—*Charles Kingsley (1819–1875)*

2
CHIVALRY

The white stallion was still sweaty from a hard day's ride. Gurion knew a little about horses—enough to know that this horse needed some care.

Wilfred made straight for the flask. "Help me off with this armor, lad."

Gurion pulled off the helmet and got his first good look at Wilfred. Emerald eyes stared out from behind the curly red of Wilfred's hair and beard. After Wilfred had explained the intricacies of removing plate armor and was free of his metallic shell, he pointed at the grazing horse.

"Comb down the steed and then join me in a draft of wine."

Gurion uncinched the white horse and removed its saddle and armor. In one of the saddlebags he found a currycomb and began combing out the day's sweat. He began to wonder what he had gotten himself into. He had come to serve the voice. Instead, he was acting as squire to a feudal knight he had just met in a place and time he could only guess.

When Gurion returned to the campsite, Wilfred was already snoring. A half loaf of dark bread lay on the empty blanket next to him. It was hard and stale, but Gurion was hungry and it tasted good. Then Gurion, too, closed his heavy eyes in sleep.

Wilfred woke Gurion before first light. "It's a long way to the manor, my lad. Wouldst thou sleep the day away?"

Gurion saw that the white stallion had already been outfitted for the day's ride. As soon as Wilfred was back in his armor they left, Wilfred on horseback and Gurion trailing behind on foot.

"Tell me about the one you serve," Gurion said.

"I serve the lord of the manor. I am one of his knights. I have pledged, on my honor, to defend him—to the death, if necessary."

"Defend him against what?"

"Roving bands of barbarians, and sometimes the knights of other lords who would increase their domain. But I am also bound to defend women and those who are defenseless. I live by the code of chivalry."

"And what is the code of chivalry?" Gurion had a pretty good idea, but he wanted to hear the knight explain it.

"It is how we are to behave. I have pledged to use my

weapons only for sacred causes. I fight for what is right and just. All forms of evil are my enemy. Against evil I will never surrender."

"How did your lord get to be a lord?"

"He is the vassal of a greater lord. He pledged his loyalty, and in return he was given possession of a small fiefdom to rule. The overlord he serves is pledged to a still greater lord."

"Can you become a lord?"

"No. I am not of noble birth. If my lord were richer I could be given a manor of my own. But that is not likely. I am his only knight."

The sun was up now, and both Wilfred and Gurion were hungry. A village lay ahead, with a patchwork of fields surrounding it. The prospect of a hearty breakfast hurried their pace.

"We will be given a friendly reception here. The lord of this village serves the same liege as my own lord does."

As Gurion and the knight approached, those guarding the walls of the village shouted to Wilfred.

"Ho! Wilfred! What brings you to the southern quarter?"

"Hunger, my friends! Give us leave to enter!"

At this the guards on the wall raised their swords as a signal and Wilfred rode through the gate with Gurion close behind. The small village was crowded miserably inside its walls. The streets, narrow and unpaved, were everywhere lined with garbage. Some of the houses were of stone, but most were built of hand-hewn boards. Nearly all the buildings were three or even four stories high. The people knelt as Wilfred passed and addressed him as "lord."

"Why do they call you lord?" Gurion whispered. "I thought you told me you were not of noble birth."

"To them, everyone above their class is a lord. They are nothing but beggars and peasants. Pay no attention to them."

Gurion thought about what Wilfred had said earlier about being bound to defend the weak and fight all forms of evil. It seemed strange that Wilfred could dismiss these people so easily, filled as they were with misery and woe. But he said nothing.

Wilfred led them to an inn of sorts. He dismounted, handed his reins to Gurion, and disappeared inside the building. Not sure exactly what he was supposed to do with the horse, Gurion was grateful when some village children offered to take care of it for him.

It was quiet in the inn. The innkeeper and his wife were talking to Wilfred, and a table was being prepared. As they ate, the talk centered around a young noblewoman named Dorothy, who had refused her betrothal to the lord's nephew and fled the village.

"She fled because she has dishonored her father," the innkeeper offered. "If you ask me, she should be hunted down and killed."

Wilfred seemed more interested in his breakfast, but he did not defend the young woman.

"And how is *your* lord fairing?" the innkeeper inquired. "Rumor has it that Dorothy wishes to marry his youngest son."

"Aye, and he would have her," Wilfred volunteered. "But that is no excuse for her to disobey her father's sacred pledge to your lord and his nephew. She is but a woman and has no right to contradict her father."

Gurion could be silent no longer. "But what of the code of chivalry? I thought you held women in the highest regard and defended their honor."

"Certainly there is no honor in the kind of disrespect the lady Dorothy has exhibited. A man's pledge is sacred," snapped Wilfred.

The innkeeper nodded in agreement, but Gurion could see that the innkeeper's wife had her doubts. Still, she was not about to dispute the matter with her husband or Wilfred. From what Gurion could tell, the innkeeper treated her more like a servant than a wife. He ordered her around roughly and did not hesitate to strike her if she failed to respond instantly to his demands.

"I tell you, that girl should be hunted down. Her father should make an example of her." The innkeeper was adamant. "We cannot have our daughters spitting in the lord's face."

Wilfred had finished his breakfast and was ready to take his leave. He sent Gurion after his mount and said his good-byes to the innkeeper.

When they had passed through the village gate and traveled down the road a way, Gurion asked somewhat hesitantly, "Do you really believe the lady Dorothy should have no right to decide whom she weds?"

"Certainly not against her lord's wishes—or her father's."

"Then what did you mean when you said that service includes being chivalrous to all the ladies? Is it chivalrous to force her into a marriage she doesn't want?"

Wilfred made no reply.

"You also said that service, according to your code, was defending the weak," Gurion continued. "Isn't it your job to defend her?"

"My job is to be faithful to my liege lord—to uphold the honor of my pledge and my lord's word."

"But can't you see that there is no honor in bullying the lady Dorothy into marrying someone she despises? Don't you have any heart at all?"

Gurion could see he was getting nowhere with Wilfred. The code of chivalry sounded so honorable—to be on the side of the weak and helpless, to fight for what was just and right, to be honor-bound by one's word and pledge. When Gurion had followed Wilfred through the door into Wilfred's world he was convinced that the code of chivalry might hold the key to understanding the true service.

Now he was not so sure. Wilfred's code ignored the peasants and dishonored women while it claimed to honor them. In reality, it was no more than a code of honor among the strong and powerful to protect their own interests.

Hours passed, and the road led once again into a forest. The heat of the early afternoon sun had turned Wilfred's tin suit into an oven, and he was grateful for the shade the forest offered. By the time they left the forest it was nearly evening. The sun was low in the sky, and a cool breeze made their journey bearable.

When they came within a few miles of Wilfred's village, Gurion could see the peasants out working the fields of the feudal lord. The crops were ripening, and some of the fields were being cut while others were being guarded against the hordes of birds that attempted to feed on the peasants' share of the harvest.

One young straw-haired boy, frustrated by the thankless and nearly impossible task of scaring the ravenous birds from the mature grain, looked longingly at the knight and his squire as they passed. Torn between his immediate task and a sense of adventure, the lad opted for adventure and ran to catch up with Wilfred and Gurion.

"I am Brainard. I offer my services, brave knight, as a page—if my lord will have me."

Wilfred laughed. "First a squire and now a page, all in the same day. We make quite a trio. I am Wilfred, sometimes called the heartless, at thy service." He winked at Gurion.

Gurion, who had not said a word to Wilfred for hours because of Wilfred's unwillingness to take up the cause of the lady Dorothy, could be angry no more. He laughed out loud and greeted Brainard with a welcoming handshake.

They soon reached the gate to Wilfred's village and made their way through the narrow streets to the manor. After the white stallion had been stabled and Wilfred's armor removed, they were called before the lord of the manor.

"Sir Wilfred, we welcome thee home. It would appear that thy quest was a successful one—that is, if an entourage was thy goal." The lord gave a passing nod to Gurion and Brainard.

"Yes, my lord."

"There have been some rather unpleasant developments of late that require immediate action."

"Yes, my lord?"

"My youngest son, Garvin, has disappeared without my leave. It seems there is a young lady, I believe her name is Dorothy, who has fled her village rather than wed someone other than Garvin. Her father is justifiably upset."

"Yes, my lord. We have just come from her village, where we heard of the unfortunate incident."

"Garvin is afraid that some ill may befall her. He asked my permission to go in search of her, but of course I denied his request. The girl is her father's to give. Had I known earlier, I might have been able to influence his decision in Garvin's favor. As it stands now, a pledge has already been made. A man's honor is at stake."

"I understand, my lord."

"I'm afraid Garvin does not. He could get himself killed if he mixes in this affair. Or, worse, he could turn the southern quarter against us. The last thing we need is trouble on that front."

"How may I be of service, my lord?"

"Go out and find Garvin before it is too late. Convince him of his folly and bring him back here."

"And the lady Dorothy, my lord?"

"I will speak to her father myself, but I doubt if there is

any honorable way out of this dilemma. A man's pledge is sacred and cannot be broken. Go now and prepare for this undertaking."

The lord had made arrangements to feed Wilfred and his attendants. Over dinner they discussed the situation they faced.

"If I know Garvin, he will head straight for the lady Dorothy's village. As soon as he makes an appearance there, any chance for cooler heads to prevail will be lost. He will be seen as the usurper, encroaching on another's territory."

"If you follow him into the southern quarter, isn't it possible that the lord might consider the village under siege?" Gurion queried.

"Yes. It is best we give our lord a chance to send his messenger to the girl's father."

"Anyway, it is obvious that Garvin seeks to avoid you." It was the voice of the young page.

Gurion was puzzled. "How do you know that?"

"Because otherwise you would have met him on the road. As you were coming from the southern quarter, Garvin was headed there. He could easily have ridden into the forest if he wished to avoid you—which is what he must have done."

"Bravo and well reasoned, my young friend!" Wilfred laughed. "Garvin is not likely to allow us to approach him, knowing that his father will surely have sent me to bring him back."

"Then I suggest we forget about Garvin, for the present, and seek the lady Dorothy instead." This time it was Gurion who spoke. "Dorothy will welcome our approach, thinking, perhaps, it is Garvin who has sent us to rescue her."

"Aye, and she will no doubt be anxious to be rescued by now." The knight followed Gurion's line of thinking. "But where do we begin to look for the lady Dorothy?"

"Everyone will assume she has come here, to Garvin's home village. Perhaps even Garvin expected to meet her on the road or find her hiding in the forest awaiting him." Gurion felt he was getting nowhere. "In fact, how do we know that he didn't find her before we ever got to the forest?"

"Because Garvin would have brought her straight back here. He has nowhere else to go." Wilfred, too, was at a dead end.

"What if the lady, knowing what everyone would expect her to do, traveled in the opposite direction—toward the enchanted forest?" The page looked pensively off into space. "I think that's what I would have done."

"The enchanted forest is no place for a lady alone. Would she dare such a thing? Even with armor and lance I shudder when I approach its dark magic." The knight paused to reflect the dire consequences of such a possibility. "And yet, the lady certainly has pluck, and it is the last place anyone would look for—"

"But if she is there, we don't have any time to lose!" Gurion interrupted.

"With fresh horses we could make it there by midnight. But we will have little luck finding her at night. No, I think it best we get a good night's sleep and start before first light."

Wilfred led his companions to his quarters and showed them to their beds. Soon, weariness overtook them all.

Even before the rooster stirred, the knight roused his troop and made ready for the day's journey. Gurion laced Wilfred into his armor and went outside to find three horses already outfitted for the day's ride.

The page visited the lord's kitchen and filled a knapsack with food and drink. Wilfred insisted on taking his lance and an extra sword, which Gurion carried, as his squire.

"We might need an extra sword in the enchanted forest. Indeed, we might need an extra swordsman!" There was no humor in Wilfred's voice.

The moon was full and allowed them enough light to give the horses their heads. They moved at a fast canter or slow gallop. By the time the sun made its appearance the horses were winded and needed a rest, but they had traveled most of the distance to the forest that separated Wilfred's village from the southern quarter. By midmorning they were passing the outskirts of the southern quarter, giving it as wide a space as possible to avoid being seen.

From Dorothy's village to the enchanted forest was less than an hour's ride. The sun was almost at its height when the entrance to the enchanted forest greeted them with an eerie mist that reminded Gurion of the island in the middle of the volcano—an island and a time that seemed centuries removed from the present moment.

Wilfred brought his horse to a halt and dismounted. "If we are correct in our reasoning, the lady Dorothy should have entered the forest here. The main road leads on to the south. The path into the forest is little traveled. With luck we may be able to pick up her trail."

The path was rocky and hard in most places, but for a short stretch, close to a natural spring, it was soft and damp. Here the hopeful search party found unmistakable boot prints leading into the forest.

"The lady has a small foot," Wilfred observed. The imprint was sharp and clear, and it was recent. "I would say the lady Dorothy is near."

As the path meandered into the forest itself a thick layer of decaying leaves made further tracking impossible. Even though it was midday, a gray mist clung tenaciously to the treetops. Still on foot, the three led their horses cautiously forward.

"It is said that dragons make their home in a cave in the midst of these woods. I don't believe the stories, but I do know of brave knights who have entered here, never to return. We must be on our guard at all times."

The path ushered them deeper into the forest. It narrowed until it was nearly indistinguishable. When it opened into a small clearing, Wilfred tied his white stallion to a tree.

"It is probably best that we leave our horses here and each take a separate direction. I don't think the lady would have gone any deeper into these woods than she had to. Brainard, stay near enough to the horses to know if anything disturbs them."

Brainard breathed a sigh of relief. "Yes, my lord. I will

comb this clearing for signs of the lady."

"Gurion, search to the east, and take my extra sword. But don't get beyond shouting distance of Brainard. I will cover the area to the west."

Gurion moved watchfully into the wild. A light breeze rustled the leaves and made a moaning sound—perhaps through some hollow tree. Behind him, he could hear Brainard calling for Dorothy and hacking his way through the brush around the perimeter of the clearing. As his senses became more alert he thought he heard the faint burble of a brook. He followed the sound and soon felt himself moving gradually downhill. At the bottom of the slope he came upon a small creek.

His instincts told him that the creek was the key to finding Dorothy. He followed it to the south for a while, and then sat down to think.

The water was clear and shallow. Gurion watched a small blue fish feeding off insects that skimmed along the creek's surface. A yellow snake slithered into the creek and moved silently toward the fish. Without thinking, Gurion blocked the snake's approach with Wilfred's sword. The fish, alerted, swam away.

Gurion decided to return to the clearing and let the others know about the creek he had found. He walked back along the creek bed but could not find the place where he had come down the slope. He yelled for Brainard, but there was no answer. He was too far from the clearing.

The wind was blowing harder now, and the moaning sound was louder. Gurion could feel his heart pounding in panic. The blood of his fear pulsed through his ears.

Suddenly he heard a splashing sound coming from the creek. He turned to see a blue fish jumping out of the water. It looked like the same fish he had saved from the snake. It started upstream, then returned, then swam upstream again. Gurion followed. Within minutes the creek forked to the left and a meadow opened before him. From the middle of the field he saw smoke. In his excitement Gurion forgot his fear. Still, he approached the fire warily, sword in hand.

It was a campfire, all right. It must have been left untended for a while, he thought, because the fire was smoldering, about to go out. However, a sizable stack of dead branches foretold the return of whoever had built it. Gurion added a branch to the fire and then sat down. He didn't have long to wait.

From the edge of the wood he saw a young woman advancing, carrying an armload of branches and twigs. She was younger than he had pictured, hardly any older than he was himself. He stood up to greet her and tried to bow gallantly. "I am Gurion, Lady Dorothy. I have come to rescue you."

The lady stood silently for a moment, taking Gurion's measure, and then she began to laugh. "You're not exactly what I expected. Who sent you? And how did you know where to find me?"

Gurion told her the whole story—about the dangerous talk in her village, and how Garvin's father had sent Wilfred out to bring back his youngest son. "We thought the best way to get Garvin's attention was to find you."

"Well, you found me. Now what?"

"I suppose we'll have to take you back to your village. But don't worry. Garvin's father promised us he will have a talk with your father."

"And my father has promised me in marriage to the lord's nephew. It means land and riches for him. And honor. There is no way he will be dissuaded. I would rather die than return to my village."

"But you can't stay here."

"What better place? Even the bravest knights are afraid of this wood. They believe it to be enchanted."

Gurion hesitated and then decided to share his absurd experience. "And suppose it is. Do you know how I found you? A fish led me to you! That sounds pretty enchanted to me."

Dorothy laughed again. "How do you know it wasn't just your imagination? You don't really believe the stories about enchantment and fire-breathing dragons, do you?"

"I don't know anymore." Gurion turned away and was silent. The wind through the trees was not as strong as it had been earlier, but he still could hear faint moaning.

"Do you want to know a secret?" Dorothy broke his reverie. "Garvin was not the real reason I ran away. He was just an excuse not to marry the lord's nephew. I think I could have loved him someday, but he was not the reason I left."

A chill ran through Gurion. Before Dorothy spoke her next words, he knew what they were going to be.

"I heard a voice," she said. "It called me into this forest. I know it sounds strange, but I am destined to be here. When I found this meadow I knew I should wait on this exact spot—for someone or something."

Gurion remembered. How could this be happening again—to him? to her? It was he, Gurion, for whom she waited. He was to lead her to the Hall of Service. But how? He didn't know how to get there himself. When he followed Wilfred through the heavy oaken door into the Middle Ages, he had assumed that the knight would lead him back when it was time.

But something told Gurion that Wilfred belonged too much to this time and this place. If Wilfred had been in the Hall, it was a dream he had long since forgotten. No, the way back was within Gurion, and him alone.

The moaning was louder now. Both he and Dorothy raised their heads to acknowledge its presence. It was a low, eerie wail that came from deep within the enchanted woods. For anyone who had a life beyond the forest it sounded a warning, a clear signal of foreboding. But Dorothy and Gurion had no place to run. For them it was a terrible beckoning, a dark summons that invited them into the very heart of enchantment itself. This time, this place, could no longer hold them. The quest to which the voice called them overcame their fears.

Afternoon was giving way to evening. And the mist that had clung to the tops of the trees was descending like the curtain at the end of a play. Dorothy looked longingly at the stacked wood, her symbol of security against the uncertainty of the forest, of life. Then Gurion took her hand and led her beyond the warm colors of the meadow into the cold gray of the forest mist.

But the drama was not yet ended. Beyond the mist, beyond the cold wind, the moaning continued to call them. It could have been the voice itself, bewailing the failure of chivalry: service so pure, so true, twisted into an evil that betrayed its very reason for existence. Service shackled and forced to promote the needs of the powerful at the expense of the weak. Evil in the garb of good.

Toward the wail of injustice they fled, deeper and deeper into the woods. The mist grew thick and sticky, like a web trying to ensnare them, contain them. But they would not be contained. Gurion cut through the mist and through the brush with Wilfred's sword. He set a furious pace, and Dorothy followed.

Finally, tattered and scratched, they reached the source of the moaning. The mouth of a large cave screamed out the wind's lament from atop an enormous bluff.

"There!" Gurion pointed at the gaping hollow in the face of the cliff. "We must hurry!"

A pattern of furrows and wrinkles in the rock would have made climbing easy were it not for the sword. Dorothy scrambled quickly to the high shelf in front of the cave and then watched Gurion's labored ascent. The sun was a red ball on the horizon when he raised himself, panting, to the ledge that decked the mouth of the cave. Dorothy pulled him safely back. From their perch, as far as they could see, the thick forest was shrouded in mist.

Gurion stood and faced the cave. With the sun directly

opposite the opening, the entire cave was aglow with a blood-red light. But it was only a matter of minutes until the sun dipped below the horizon.

The moaning reverberated, as if some giant beast were awakening. Great sinister shadows moved on the back wall as Dorothy and Gurion took their first steps inside the cavern. Gurion clutched Wilfred's sword and swallowed hard. Tales of enchantment and fire-breathing dragons spun around in his mind and riveted his feet to the floor of the cave. His world began to spin. "No! Not here, not now."

Dorothy took his arm and led him forward. The center of the cave was flat and clear. Gurion knelt against the cold stone and bowed his head to clear it of dizziness. Already the glow that illuminated the cave was beginning to diminish.

"Are you all right?"

Gurion nodded. From his knees he surveyed the monstrous room. To the left were boulders and rough columns whose extended shadows cast a menagerie of grotesque shapes behind them. The center of the cave was clear—too clear, almost as if it had been emptied of debris and its floor polished. To the right, the floor of the cave sloped down and disappeared from view. The groaning was coming from the direction of the slope.

"This way." Gurion grabbed Dorothy's hand and pulled her along with him.

The descending ramp soon turned into rough stairs, which spiraled down the perimeter of the cave. As the sun set, the cave darkened until it was nearly impossible for them to see anything. Still, Gurion and Dorothy inched forward, feeling their way along the wall, testing every step.

The wind continued to blow outside, and the low wail, bellowing up from deep in the earth, guided their advance.

Then, without warning, Gurion stopped. The wall of the cave, which up to this point had been rough and jagged, had suddenly become smooth and polished to the touch. He pushed against the stone and it yielded, opening into a lighted passageway. As they entered, Gurion felt a familiar rumble.

"The twilight gate?" he said incredulously.

Dorothy looked at him with questioning eyes, but Gurion had no time to explain.

"If that sound is what I think it is, we have fifteen minutes to find the twilight gate; otherwise we will be stuck here until morning."

The way was well lighted, with torches burning every few steps to show the way. Gurion and Dorothy hurried down the tunnel, which opened eventually into the great room. As they approached the runway of lights that led to the twilight gate, a rumble shook the floor.

Gurion shouted ahead to Dorothy, who had taken the lead. "Hurry, the drawbridge is being raised!"

Dorothy reached the bridge just in time to jump across the widening gap. By the time Gurion got there the gap had widened to a couple of paces. He tried to get himself to jump, but he remembered the bottomless pit and froze in his tracks. All he could do was watch as the bridge raised itself into a vertical tower.

From across the precipice Dorothy called to him.

"Gurion, what happened? Why didn't you jump?"

Before Gurion could answer, he saw a familiar face behind Dorothy. "Kendra!"

"Welcome, my friend. I see Dorothy made it just in time."

A little startled, Dorothy turned to face the old woman.

"I will take you the rest of the way to the Hall of Service. I am Kendra, the gatekeeper."

Dorothy looked one last time at Gurion, trapped on the other side of the twilight gate.

"Don't worry about me, I'll be fine," he said, trying to assure both Dorothy and himself.

He watched them disappear down the lighted path and then remembered that the lights in the great room were on a timer. He didn't want to spend the night in a pitch black cavern, so he scrambled to find the torch-lined tunnel. He found it just as the lights of the great room were extinguished.

And if I have prophetic powers, and understand all mysteries and all knowledge, and if I have all faith, so as to remove mountains, but do not have love, I am nothing. If I give away all my possessions, and if I hand over my body so that I may boast, but do not have love, I gain nothing. . . . And now faith, hope, and love abide, these three; and the greatest of these is love.

−1 Cor. 13:2-3, 13

3

CHARITY

Gurion could not possibly have prepared Dorothy for the Hall of Service. Like Gurion, she had been drawn there by some irresistible force that had called her out of her feudal world—a force more powerful than the rigid institutions that try to shape the lives of women and men in any particular time or place.

Yet in many ways Dorothy was a product of the late Middle Ages, even though she had revolted against some of its customs and practices. The idea that she was of secondary importance—that her wishes and needs were forfeit anytime they conflicted with those of husband, lord, or father—was ingrained in her.

As she stood before the majesty of the Hall she felt a mixture of awe, inadequacy, and guilt. Who was she to be in this great Hall? How did she have the courage to go against father and lord?

She watched as representatives from times and places unimaginable talked and carried out their business. She watched and she waited, unsure of her role there, wondering if she was experiencing reality or dream, life or death.

Her stay in the small room had been brief. She had barely had time to focus on the strange arch of letters, MINISTRARE EST VIVERE, before she gave herself up to the force that had drawn her there. *Ministrare est vivere.* She knew it was Latin, probably some kind of motto—a guiding principle for the Hall.

Kendra had told her that time had no significance here. She wondered what that could mean.

The Hall was so large, and there was so much that she did not understand. Suddenly it all seemed overwhelming. She felt herself drifting, staggering under the weight of all that had happened. Fatigue gripped her and sapped her strength. She had to find a place to sit—no, to lie down.

Behind her, between the oaken door and its strange statue, she saw a stone bench. She made her way to the bench and reclined on its cold, hard surface. It felt good to close her eyes. The voices in the busy Hall grew fainter. She felt herself floating away, to sleep, to dream.

It was the past, or perhaps the future. A chorus of people in pastel robes appeared before her with a halo of unfocused light around them. They were speaking in unison about someone she had no knowledge of, describing someone important to her for reasons as yet unclear:

There was nothing attractive about her, no dignity or beauty to make us take notice. She seemed somehow disfigured. Everything was a struggle for her, every move she made, every sound she uttered. She spoke words we could not understand and danced some kind of inhuman dance every time she tried to walk. We were shocked and embarrassed by her presence. We made fun of her behind her back and hated the sight of her. When she was with us we ignored her as if she were nothing. No one would even look at her.

One of the people in the crowd, a woman in a blue robe, stepped forward and confessed through tears of pain:

I tell you this now with great shame. Had I known then what I now know about her, I would have treated her differently. I would have stood up for her and been a friend. I would have tried harder to understand the words she struggled to speak. It would have been different. Or at least I like to think it would have been different. And yet, perhaps even knowing, I would have rejected her. It could be—and this is the most painful thought of all—that I did know. Somewhere in the depths of my soul I must have known.

The chorus spoke again, in unison:

There was nothing attractive about her then. She was an object of ridicule and scorn. She was different. And that was enough to make us hate her. We thought of her as some kind of freak, a creature even nature had rejected.

A man in a yellow robe spoke next:

But she was not a freak. She was a human being. If she was in some ways different from us, she was in more ways our sister. She felt the same warm sun and cool breeze. She knew the same fears, the same hopes. She wanted to be loved and to love.

Again the chorus spoke:

We saw only her outward appearance, and that through the distorted lens of prejudice. We did not see who she was; or, if we did see, it frightened us so much we were blinded by our fear.

A woman in a purple robe spoke:

She was good. And that in itself was enough to make her seem a freak. She was good in ways I have never known before or since. I wonder now if it was this good in her that made her seem disfigured.

The chorus:

Did we see, perhaps, our own twisted reflection in the mirror her life presented to us?

A man in green:

It is difficult now, looking back, to see her as I saw her then. Having experienced her goodness, my perception of her is transformed. *Beyond those differences that frightened and offended me, I see now her unique beauty and perfection. The words I could not or would not understand penetrate to my very being. The way she moved, which seemed then repulsive, became a measure of her courage, her dance as wonderful as any ballerina.*

Again, the chorus spoke:

We despised her and rejected her; because of us she endured suffering and pain. We would not see past her disabilities to her special gifts. We were blind to her unique genius, deaf to the ideas she tried to contribute. Our prejudice crippled us.

Finally, a woman in orange said softly:

She never said a word against us. She thought of us as her friends. Can you imagine that? In spite of the way we treated her, she chose to see the good in us.

The chorus began to blur and fade away:

We ignored her as if she were nothing. Not one of us would even look at her. . . .

Dorothy awoke with a start. The background of voices that had spoken to her in her dream became again the voices of the crowd in the Hall of Service—all speaking their own separate conversations. Then a more familiar voice addressed her from the foot of the bench.

"I wondered if I would be able to find you. It has been nearly a week since we got separated." It was Gurion.

"A week? No, that is impossible. I only rested here for a moment."

"Yes, but you must remember that this is the Hall of Service. Space and time have no meaning here."

Dorothy rubbed her eyes and sat up. "And what *does* have meaning? I just dreamed the strangest dream—a crowd of people remembering someone they had wronged. It was as if they were confessing their sins to me. There was so much pain."

"I don't know what dreams mean in here. It all seems like a dream to me. The only thing I know for sure is that everything that happens teaches us something—something about service." Gurion smiled. "Everyone in this Hall is here for the same reason. And we are all learning at our own pace."

"Where do all the doors lead?" Dorothy asked. "I thought Kendra said there was only one way into the Hall."

Gurion paused to reflect. "The oaken door behind us leads into your world. It's the only door I've tried so far. I'm told that the others lead into every imaginable time and place. And every door has a lesson to teach us."

"What made you choose the door into my world?"

"I followed Wilfred." Gurion laughed. "He sort of bumped into me here."

Dorothy was skeptical. "Wilfred? Here in the Hall? It doesn't seem possible."

"Perhaps he stumbled in, somehow, without knowing where he was. Or perhaps he was called to lead me into his world. I don't know. But once back in his world, all memory of the Hall was soon forgotten. He never spoke of it."

"If I went back through the oaken door, do you suppose that I, too, would forget the Hall of Service and the voice that called me here?" Dorothy wondered aloud.

"I think maybe that's exactly what happens if we go back to our own worlds through these doors. Kendra says she will lead us back into our world when we know the true service. She says our quest here is a pursuit of that true service."

Just then a woman in a pink robe darted across the Hall. Dorothy sprang to her feet and started running after her. "Gurion, it's her! One of the women from my dream! I've got to catch up with her."

Gurion chased behind, excusing himself as he made his way through the crowd. Every now and then he caught a glimpse of the woman in pink. She moved hurriedly down the length of the Hall, with Dorothy gaining on her. By the time Gurion caught up with Dorothy, the woman in the pink robe had disappeared through a door marked MC23.

"I didn't even get a chance to speak with her," Dorothy said. "She was in such a hurry."

Gurion could see the disappointment on her face. "Come on," he said. "Let's explore the Hall. Whoever she was, she didn't want to speak with you."

But Dorothy was not about to be dissuaded. She gave Gurion one last glance and then opened door MC23.

Gurion hesitated and then followed her into the glare of an afternoon sun.

Beyond the door it was cold and windy. The ground in front of them was rocky and bare. Dorothy was shading her eyes from the glare, trying to locate the mysterious pink-robed stranger from out of her dream. She looked back to see Gurion stepping through what appeared to be a perfectly symmetrical opening in the rock. As soon as he was completely through the opening, it closed, leaving no trace in the wall of stone.

Seconds, perhaps minutes, passed before either Dorothy or Gurion said a word. The landscape was bleak and strange to them. They seemed to be part of the way up a mountain, but there were no trees or plants anywhere. There were no clouds in the sky, and the sun was fiercely bright, yet it was a cold sun, a winter sun.

To the south a valley wound its way for leagues through the rocky hills and peaks of some unknown mountain range. The valley was filled with drifts of fluffy white—like a great frozen river covered with a snowy mantle. To the north and west, as far as the eye could see, the blanket of white was unbroken. The only way open to them appeared to be up an eastern trail that led to the top of the mountain.

Gurion probed the rocky wall behind him, seeking a way back into the Hall. But he knew it was no use. The only way into the Hall was through the twilight gate.

Dorothy had begun to walk down the path that led to the snowy blanket. "She went this way, Gurion. I'm sure of it."

Only seconds had elapsed between the time the woman in pink left the Hall and Dorothy and Gurion followed. But seconds in the Hall could mean hours or even days in this strange world.

Gurion looked again at the peaks rising out of the snow. Something was wrong. Even the tallest peaks were bare of snow or ice. Why would the peaks be bare and the valleys filled with snow? Gurion studied the white drifts more closely.

"Clouds!" he muttered to himself. "We're above the clouds!"

Dorothy was already moving quickly down the path. Gurion sighed. Clouds, at least, were no barrier to their descent. He hurried to catch up before she disappeared into the mist.

The way down was steep, but the path was well worn and easily passable. For hours they trudged through the sticky mist, until finally they had broken through its damp obscurity into the waiting world beneath.

They were still perhaps halfway up the mountain. Below them they could see a broad green valley punctuated by farms and a medium-sized village.

Evening was approaching rapidly. It would soon be too dark to continue. The clouds gave them a measure of protection against the cold, but they needed shelter. Gurion was tired. Dorothy had not slowed her pace or spoken a word since they began their descent. She seemed driven by some urgency—like a bloodhound on the scent. Suddenly she stopped.

"Here! I can feel it. She went off the trail here."

There did seem to be a path of sorts leading away from the main trail. It was rocky and steep, but before long it led them to some carefully constructed steps that made the going much easier. At the bottom of the steps the path leveled. A wide, flat plain spread out before them, a hidden valley protected by three separate peaks. A portion of the plain was forested, and a cluster of simple huts stood backed up against the trees.

As they approached the tiny hamlet, Gurion could see movement. A rainbow of pastel robes hurried this way and that, gathering and stowing and preparing for the night.

Dorothy did not pause. She ran toward the hooded figures as if they were long-lost friends. A man in a lavender robe greeted her with a gesture of welcome. Then a second figure, a woman in orange, stopped what she was doing and offered Dorothy her two open hands like a sister. Dorothy took hold of the outstretched hands and then knelt before her.

Gurion watched from outside the circle of huts. Not a word had been spoken. Yet much had been experienced. Somehow Dorothy knew without being told that the spoken word had been banished here. She turned to Gurion, her eyes flooded with empathy, and raised an index finger to her lips. Gurion understood. He entered the circle and was welcomed with a nod and a smile.

The evening campfire was being prepared. Dead wood gleaned from the forest was stored in a huge mound. Food was offered to the visitors, and they were given robes.

First the setting of the sun was celebrated in a simple vigil. Then the ritual fire was lit. Gurion and Dorothy watched in silence as the hands of the villagers danced in the flicker of the firelight, telling tales long remembered, tales too sacred to be spoken or heard.

When the evening's ceremonies had ended, Dorothy and Gurion were led to the hut of the woman in the orange robe. It was little more than a shelter, unadorned by furniture or decorations. All that graced the floor were a half dozen straw-filled mats. Once inside the hut, the precious silence was broken.

"We have been waiting for you to arrive," the orange-robed woman said softly. "Panya told us you were coming."

"Panya?" Dorothy asked.

"Yes, Panya is a prophet. She had a vision, a dream, in which you appeared. My name is Olena. I have been given the great honor to serve you."

"By any chance does Panya wear a pink robe?" Gurion asked.

Startled, Olena took a long look at Gurion. "Yes, she does. How did you know?"

"Let's just say she came to us in her dream." Gurion knew that since Panya had reentered her world through the door in the Hall of Service, she would have no memory of the Hall.

"My name is Dorothy, and my friend is Gurion."

Olena knelt and kissed the hems of their robes.

"I, too, had a dream . . . about your people. I am here because of that dream." Dorothy didn't know exactly how to begin.

"My people are known as the sons and daughters of charity," Olena explained. "We live apart from the world because we have much to remember, and the world is a place of forgetfulness."

Olena offered straw mats to Dorothy and to Gurion. When they were comfortable, she continued. "It all began a long time ago. Would you like to hear our story?"

Dorothy nodded. "It is why we have come."

"Do you know the language of dancing hands, the language of sign?"

Gurion and Dorothy looked at each other. It was Gurion who spoke. "Where I come from there is a sign language used by people who are deaf. It is a beautiful language of gestures and hand symbols, but I have never learned it."

"The only way I know the story of my people is through the language of dancing hands. We never speak the story out loud to one another; it would be considered rude. In fact, we never use our voices at all beyond the walls of our dwellings. But that is part of the story."

"I think I know a little of your story," Dorothy said. "Some of your people, including Panya, came to me in a dream. There was much pain. Something about a young woman who was disfigured—"

"No!" Olena interrupted. "It is true we thought her disfigured, but she was more than we could ever be. She was touched by God."

"But you rejected her?"

"Yes. We did not understand. She was different, and we had been taught to hate what was different, or at least to fear it."

Gurion cleared his throat. "Would you mind starting from the beginning? I don't know any of the story, and I am confused."

Olena smiled. "We tell the story every night in the language of dancing hands. You witnessed it tonight, but our signs and gestures are meaningless to those who are untrained in the language."

"Can you tell us the story in words?" Gurion asked.

She hesitated. "Yes, but it cannot be repeated outside these walls. Do you understand?" Olena waited for both Dorothy and Gurion to acknowledge her question. "And you must keep in mind that I am translating the story into a language that is unworthy of it. It was never intended to be spoken or heard."

In the dim light of the single lantern that burned on the floor between them, Gurion and Dorothy could see Olena's hands begin to dance. Only after she saw the story on her fingers could she share it with them in words. It was as if the memory of the story was carried in her hands themselves.

A long time ago, in the village of Weeping Oak, a child was born. She was born to a very poor family who had to beg in order to keep from starving. As the girl grew up she learned to beg for her food in the eastern section, near the old oak tree that was the village namesake.

Now this ancient oak was hundreds of years old. And for as long as anyone could remember it bore a strange disease that made it weep sap from a variety of wounds, but especially from two holes that looked like eyes and formed a kind of face high up on the aged trunk.

Cara—for that was the girl's name—loved the ancient tree and played in its branches whenever she was not begging for food. The tree seemed to respond to her affection, for it stopped its weeping. Most of its wounds healed over with new bark, and its "eyes" grew clear and bright.

Then one day Cara did not come to the tree. Some of the villagers noticed her absence, but she was only a beggar child and of no consequence to them. Days grew into weeks, and weeks into months, and still Cara did not come. Finally, she returned. But she had been changed.

When the tree saw her it began to weep again. Some say it wept tears of pain, others insist they were tears of joy. But Cara could no longer climb the tree and play in its branches. She had been very ill with a high fever. For weeks she had hovered between life and death, and when her fever finally broke and she began to recover, something had been taken from her—and something given.

The fever had burned into her brain and damaged the nerves that controlled her legs. When she tried to walk she danced some kind of inhuman dance. Her speech was also affected. It was a struggle for her to make her mouth form words. And when she uttered them they could not be understood. Her hearing, too, was gone. Not a sound could penetrate her new silence.

To the villagers she was some kind of freak, a child to be pitied. She was flooded with alms, but no one would go near her. She was the object of ridicule and scorn. Even the other beggars of the village laughed at her and made coarse jokes. She was an outcast, a pariah.

Every day she made her way painfully and laboriously to the old tree. She sat at the base of its broad trunk. The good people of the village filled her basket because they pitied her. And the tree wept.

Everyone saw what had been taken from her. Some of us pitied her and gave her a measure of our good fortune. Others of us laughed at her and mocked her.

None of us saw what had been given to her.

Olena paused to swallow the lump that was welling up in her throat. Even in the dim light, Dorothy and Gurion could see tears streaming down her face.

The fever had nearly taken Cara's life. It had robbed her of her coordination, her speech, her hearing. It had left her an object of pity. Bereft of friends, destitute, abandoned by all but the weeping oak, she might easily have grown bitter and hateful. But she did not. The One who had rescued her from the deadly fever had touched her. Her losses were great, but the gifts she had been given were greater by far.

Years passed. Cara taught herself the language of dancing hands. There were two others in the village who could not speak or hear. Cara practiced her gestures and hand symbols with them until she could be understood by them.

She had so much to share with the village, but none of the hearing people could understand her. She tried to communicate through words, but no one would take the trouble to understand her. She gained a reputation as the village idiot.

We know now what she was trying to share. When we

learned the language of dancing hands, the two who shared her knowledge of the language explained what she had been trying to tell us. The fever that had stolen her speech and hearing had affected some other nerves as well. Or, perhaps it was the touch of the One who healed her. Who can say?

She had been given a rare gift. Her sense of sight had somehow been connected with what she smelled and tasted. She saw shapes and colors when she tasted food. Designs accompanied scents and fragrances. For years we thought these gifts were unique to her, but we have since learned of others who possess them.

Her greatest gift, however, was her ability to love. In spite of all our pity, our scorn and ridicule, our malice and spite, she never said a word against us. She thought of us as her friends. And when the time of our great need came, she didn't hesitate for a moment.

Again Olena had to pause to compose herself. She got up from her mat and walked slowly around the room. When she returned her voice was firm and strong.

A plague settled on our village. Two plagues, really, with similar symptoms, but requiring drastically different treatments. The medication that would relieve the symptoms of one could be fatal in the case of the other. Our doctors were terrified of prescribing the wrong medicine, and yet to prescribe no medicine at all was equally dangerous. Both plagues were extremely contagious. Everyone had to be treated in an attempt to stop the spread of death and destruction before it claimed the whole village.

Cara watched as both her parents were treated—only to see them die. She could not possibly have understood the problem involved in determining the right medication, because no one could have told her. And yet, when the doctors were about to administer what they hoped was the right drug to save her younger brother, Cara stopped them. She tasted the drug and then waved her arms frantically and shook her head. She ran and got some of the drug that had killed her parents and held it out to the physicians. When they did not respond, she fed it to her brother.

The doctors were unable to stop her. And once the medicine had been given it was impossible to undo the damage. The doctors were certain it was just a matter of time until the boy died. But Cara's brother did not die. Within hours he was showing signs of recovery.

Somehow, Cara was able to match the right medicine to each disease—something the doctors could not do. Word of what she had done spread around the village faster than the plague itself. People demanded her presence when the risky choice of medications was made. She never failed.

We know now that her special gift enabled her to match the unique design of the scent of each disease to the colors and shapes she saw when she tasted the different medications. She was tireless in her efforts to save the people of the village. She worked day and night with the physicians. Thousands of lives were saved.

Then, just as the terrible tide was turning and there was hope again for the village of Weeping Oak, Cara came down with both diseases simultaneously. Her weakened resistance and continued exposure had made her vulnerable. There was nothing *anyone could do for her.*

She was buried next to the old oak tree she loved so much. It is said the tree still weeps at the mention of her name.

Dorothy and Gurion stared silently at the shadows cast by the flickering lantern. They thought about the countless Caras in the world–the poor and the downtrodden who were seen by the world as nobodies, objects of pity and scorn. They pondered the unnamed gifts wasted because the world placed so little value on lives weakened by poverty, disability, old age. Olena, too, was silent for a long time. Then she spoke.

After Cara's death, a number of us realized we had been changed by her life. We saw our village drifting back into its old destructive patterns. Beggars still roamed the streets, receiving jeers as often as handouts. Even Cara's brother, who had recovered from his illness only to be cast out into the streets as an orphan, was taunted and ridiculed.

Those of us who could not forget Cara's gift of love formed a community that came to be known as the sons and daughters of charity. We donned robes that blushed with the colors of our hope–the colors of Cara's special vision that had allowed her to save our village. We learned the language of dancing hands and preserved Cara's memory in a nightly ritual that told her story in her own language. We opened our community to rich and poor, to strong and weak, to people of diverse gifts and challenges.

But the village of Weeping Oak saw us as a threat. Some of our houses were burned to the ground as a warning. One of our leaders was taken to the ancient oak and stoned to death. Our colored robes became targets for the hatred and bigotry that burned in the hearts of a few disgruntled souls who misunderstood our intent. We were forced to flee the village.

Providence led us to this protected spot, halfway up the mountain. Our community has fared well here. And though our colors are still not welcome in the village below, we have managed to bring hope to the hearts of some who would otherwise have no hope. The discards of the village occasionally find their way to us when their burdens become more than they can bear.

It was late when the story was done. Olena extinguished the lantern so the three of them would sleep. But Dorothy and Gurion could not rest yet. They talked most of the night about the plight of the sons and daughters of charity.

Somehow this community had become a symbol of charity itself. Charity. How sadly it was misunderstood by the world. It was despised and rejected by some, distorted and cheapened by others. Charity—an idea feared and even hated by good people who had no room in their hearts for the needs of the weak and the powerless.

But what did charity have to do with the quest for true service? Why had they been led to this community to hear Cara's story?

Both Gurion and Dorothy had been brought up in societies that understood charity as help or alms given to the poor and unfortunate. Charity was the responsibility of the powerful to the downtrodden. It was an act of kindness and generosity that left the poor indebted, beholden. To accept charity invited a stigma that proud people found so distasteful and disgraceful that some would rather starve than receive it.

Now charity was being redefined for them. Charity was a state of mind. Yes, it could involve sharing alms with the poor. But it invited the poor to share their gifts as well. Indeed, it allowed for the possibility that the poor might have important gifts to share.

Charity was an attitude, an attitude of goodwill and respect. It refused the notion of "somebodies" and "nobodies." It brought humanity together in a common bond. It shattered the lie that some of us can provide for ourselves without the help of others.

When the first rays of morning finally broke between the mountain peaks and colored the sky with the hope of a new day, Dorothy and Gurion rose from their mats and greeted Olena with tired smiles.

"You missed the morning ceremonies," Olena informed them. "I didn't have the heart to wake you. Here is your breakfast."

Olena set two generous bowls of hot cereal before them and then excused herself to fulfill her morning duties.

"I think we've learned what we came to learn," Gurion said. "I suppose it is time for us to try to find our way back to the Hall. My guess is the top of the mountain."

But Dorothy resisted. "You can go back if you want. I'm going to stay. I have to go down to the village. I don't know why, exactly. But I must see the old oak tree."

The village. It invited and repelled Gurion. There was

something about the ancient tree that called out to him as it called out to Dorothy. But he was afraid. He watched, without finding any words to explain or defend his fear, as Dorothy finished her cereal and then went outside to say her good-byes.

In silence she hugged Olena and then started back up the path that led to the main trail.

God blessed them [the human beings], and God said to them, "Be fruitful and multiply, and fill the earth and subdue it; and [have] dominion over the fish of the sea and over the birds of the air and over every living thing that moves upon the earth."

–Gen. 1:28

4
DOMINION

A solitary figure in a pale yellow robe resolutely approached the village of Weeping Oak. She had covered a distance of nearly seven leagues in just under five hours of steady walking. Weary and craving food and drink, she pushed herself relentlessly, determined to permit herself rest only when she was at the foot of the ancient oak.

Dorothy had looked for Gurion to follow her. She knew that he, too, had been moved by the story Olena had told. For hours she had squinted back up the trail behind her, expecting to see the green of his robe. Finally she had stopped looking for him.

As she neared the village, she began to meet people on the road. But even though she smiled and greeted them, neither her smiles nor her greetings were returned. She was obviously an unwelcome intruder, but she didn't understand why. Stare after cold stare pierced her like poisoned daggers until she learned to avoid eye contact entirely and walked with her eyes lowered.

By the time she reached the village streets she had been ridiculed and spat on a number of times. Even small children jeered at her and called her names. But her determination never wavered. She made her way toward the center of town, where Olena had said the old tree stood.

Finally she saw the great crown of its branches. Her eyes filled with tears, and she quickened her pace. This was Cara's tree, the weeping oak that had held Cara in its branches and shared her pain.

The tree was even bigger than Dorothy had imagined. Its gnarled branches spread in every direction. The huge trunk that supported the weight of so many years was crusted with dried sap that had run down from two circles, which stared like eyes at its uppermost point.

The circles, which were hollows from lost branches pruned away centuries ago, had wept themselves closed. They were caked shut with a hard yellow resin, so that the tree appeared to have been blinded.

Dorothy placed her hands against the tree to feel its life, but felt nothing. No breeze stirred its limbs. No birds made their nests in its branches. It could have been some grotesque clay statue standing in a world that knew nothing of trees, or of tears wept in sorrow.

Pain as harsh as winter had forced everything vital to be withdrawn, pulled so deep within the tree that no spring could call it forth. The tree stood dormant, a spiritless monument to what once had been.

The energy Dorothy had sought to bolster her own sagging spirits was lacking. The old oak had nothing to give. She slumped to the ground at the base of the tree in utter exhaustion.

"Oh, Cara," she said softly. "What has happened to our world?"

A subtle mound of earth marked what must have been Cara's grave. Littered with the garbage of passing villagers, it was forgotten, abandoned—except for a blanket of shade, the gift of the oak's gnarled branches.

After a few minutes' rest, Dorothy roused herself enough to clean the mound of the villagers' careless discards. She raked its mantle of soil lovingly with her fingers until it was clean and smooth. Then she carried a large flat rock to mark the site. When she had finished she collapsed beside the grave and began to sob uncontrollably.

"You gave so much to be remembered so little."

As her tears watered the ground, some inner wind moved the ancient oak's branches. A faint rustle broke the tree's long silence. Something stirred within its broad trunk. Dorothy heard the tree creak and moan. Chunks of crusted sap cracked and fell away. Leaves, curled shut from the tree's long dormancy, spread open slightly as the tree stretched and yawned itself awake.

Again Dorothy placed her hands on the tree. This time her fingers felt a pulse of life. The great tree trembled at her touch. Its bark twisted and pulled against the stiffness of a generation of inactivity. More clumps of dried sap fell away.

Dorothy felt her own senses awakening. Something in

her responded to the great tree's struggle to break the chains of abuse and neglect that had sent it retreating so deeply into itself. There was more buried here than just the special memory of Cara's life. The ancient oak had begun its weeping centuries before Cara had played under its branches.

The old tree was rooted in the land, and there was pain and sorrow abroad that ran deep. Dorothy felt the tree's pain, the great sorrow of the land. Her fingers read the oak's history as if it were written in braille, as if the crusted sap were some kind of alphabet for the unrooted—for those, like Dorothy, who were blind to what was happening.

Images flashed into Dorothy's mind: images of the land's health and vigor being attacked by greed and egoism, images as fragmented and disjointed as the flaking sap itself. She did not understand what she saw. Somehow she had to get closer to the living tree.

She pulled gently at the crusted old deposits that had accumulated from years and years of weeping. Every touch conjured up ghastly pictures in her mind, and every picture screamed with pain. She hoped that by removing the lacquered layers of injury she would free the tree and enable it to breathe new life once again.

Painstakingly, she picked and scraped away the hardened residue, cleaning the trunk from its base to the two knotholes that had wept the sap.

But she was afraid to remove the yellow resin from the hollow sockets that stared blindly back at her. Even without touching them she could feel the immensity of their pain. An aura of grief radiated from eyes that were not eyes, bestowing a terrifying vision of the land to one who had eyes and yet was blind.

Through the great oak's vitality, Dorothy found herself rooted in the soil, grafted to a memory that was hundreds of years old. She had called the living sap back from its winter of despair; now she would share its insight into the land's sorrow.

Dorothy could not locate her vision in chronological time. She felt instinctively that she was older than the tree, that she had come from a time distant and past all remembering. The story of the land that she had tapped into was the story of a future remote and almost beyond her understanding.

The vision was brief but powerful. Dorothy pulled back. She was weeping and did not know exactly why. She looked down at her robe and saw the land's sickly yellow colors reflected in it. A flash of rootedness, a moment's insight, changed forever the way she viewed the earth and her place on it.

High atop the mountain, Gurion gazed down through broken clouds on the village of Weeping Oak. His fear had sent him here, as far from the ancient tree as he could get. Yet there was no escape for him on the mountain, and somewhere deep inside he knew it. Even at this great distance, all his attention was focused on the tree. It awaited him. There was no way out but through the valley of his fear.

Olena had sensed his dread. When he had tried to

return the green robe she had refused him. What use had he of robes the color of hope? He was going back, not down. But Olena knew, somehow, that back *was* down—down wearing the robe of charity.

So Gurion sat in his green robe, measuring the strength of his resistance. He could not take his eyes off the village below. Strangely, the mountaintop held no power, no answers. This time the answers were rooted deep in the earth. And Gurion knew that it was not just Cara's earth, it was his as well.

The roots of the ancient oak ran deep. Bitter waters past and present fed its tears. He knew intuitively that it was not Cara's history it wept over but his own.

He had wasted a lot of time following the trail up to the mountaintop. Now, even if he pushed himself to the limit, he doubted he could make it to the village before dark. He could go back to the community of hope and spend another night there, but that would only delay what he knew now was inevitable.

Gurion reflected on his place in this troubled world. He had come from a moment in history when human beings completely dominated and subdued nature. Science and technology had finally made it possible for people to control the environment, to reap huge profits from an enslaved planet.

But utter dominion left a wake of consequences. Permanent rain forests were burned or bulldozed to create temporary grazing land where cheap beef could be raised for fast-food restaurants. Millions of years of petroleum deposits were squandered in a fifty-year energy frenzy that changed the makeup of the atmosphere. A seemingly endless supply of timber was harvested for lumber and paper products at the expense of forest animals and future generations of human beings. Garbage and toxic waste polluted the world's oceans and seeped into water tables from landfills unable to digest the gluttonous debris of a consumer society. Chemicals, thought necessary to improve the quality of human life, destroyed the protective ozone layer and left all of life more vulnerable to disease and radiation.

This, then, was the legacy of Gurion's generation, and of his parents and grandparents. Gurion knew well why the great oak wept. He knew that in facing the tree's pain he would be facing his own guilt.

That guilt weighed heavily on him as Gurion pulled himself to his feet and started down the mountain. Everywhere he looked he saw evidence of the land's bondage. Mountaintops that should have been green with plant life were barren and lifeless. What vegetation remained was lacking in vitality and colored a sickly yellow. Animals were almost entirely absent; an eerie silence bore mute testimony to their loss. No birds sang. No squirrels chattered. Only the buzz of insects broke the stillness.

As Gurion walked, he became more and more aware of the great losses the world had sustained. In his wildest nightmares he had never imagined a future beyond technology, beyond the scientific improvements he had taken for granted in the late twentieth century. Could this, indeed, be a future time? It seemed impossible. *Future* was a word that had always implied "better" to him. It was a word filled with promise and hope. Now it appeared that promise and hope had been betrayed.

It was late evening when Gurion reached the foot of the mountain. The moon was full and the clouds had dissipated, giving him just enough light to see. He followed the road toward the village.

Even at this late hour, farmers tended their fields. Without the aid of animal or machine, they tried to coax sweet corn and other grains from an embittered soil. The sight of Gurion in his green robe seemed to infuriate them.

"Go back up the mountain, you freeloader! We have nothing to give you. We *work* for our food!"

Gurion tried to explain that the robe was a gift, that he did not belong to the community of hope. But no one would allow him to approach. Some even cast stones at him and laughed when he cried out in pain.

By the time he finally reached the village, his legs aching from leagues of walking, the townspeople were asleep in their beds. The streets were empty and quiet. No dogs barked as he walked toward the center of town, because there were no dogs. No trees lined the streets.

Gurion wondered if Dorothy had received the same belligerent welcome that he had experienced. He began to worry about her. Olena had spoken of terrible things happening in the village. Some who dared to wear the robes of hope here had been stoned to death.

By Gurion's calculations, Dorothy must have entered the

village in the middle of the day. A mob of people would have been there to greet her, to take out their frustrations on her. He shuddered at the thought and hurried toward the center of town, toward the weeping oak.

He found it more easily than he had expected, its lone branches silhouetted against the face of the moon. Gurion approached the tree with reverence and knelt at its base.

It was not because Gurion thought the tree harbored some great spirit that he knelt. Even though he had been moved by the stories about the tree, he did not believe that the ancient oak possessed the human qualities attributed to it. Gurion knelt because he respected the tree and what it symbolized. God made this tree. It belonged to a world God created and pronounced good. That was reason enough to treat it with respect, to dignify it with the most profound honor.

In the midst of a nature ravaged by human beings who had set themselves up as greedy demigods stood this ancient tree. Somehow it had survived their polluted worldview. Its weeping sap was evidence that it suffered from a disease attributable to the profaning of the earth. Yet it had survived.

Like Gurion it was robed in a mantle of green, cloaked with the color of hope. Gurion responded to that hope. Perhaps it was not too late for healing. Perhaps the future that had been betrayed could be redeemed.

There was a brokenness that spread throughout every dimension of this world, a need for healing on many levels. Charity had been banished, love rejected and denied. If there had ever been anything like a conscience toward the land, it had been forgotten. In order for healing to take place, at least as far as the earth was concerned, this long-forgotten conscience toward the land had to be revived.

It is hard to say whether or not Gurion understood any of this. But he knew guilt. He knew—though he couldn't put it into words—that he could not separate himself from the responsibility his generation shared for the profaning of the earth. Gurion felt guilt toward the land and toward this magnificent oak. He didn't know what he could do to make amends for his part in the tragedy, but he accepted his guilt and wanted to do something.

And so he knelt.

The tree did not stir. If it had been moved by Gurion's gesture of reconciliation, no human eye could have measured its reaction. But Gurion was moved. At the foot of the great oak, he thought about the voice that had called him to serve.

What did it mean to serve the voice? Certainly he had served when he answered the call and made his way to the island. But the voice wasn't just taking attendance. He had been called for a reason, a purpose. Service involved commitment. He was learning that it involved preparation, understanding, and participation as well.

He had followed the knight, Wilfred, because he thought the age of chivalry would teach him true service, but chivalry's noble ideals had been perverted to serve the interests of the rich and powerful.

Perhaps it was the concern for the poor and downtrodden awakened in him by Wilfred's world that had led him to follow Dorothy into *this* world. His understanding of charity had been greatly changed here. The prevailing view, one he had always assumed to be correct, turned out to be a disservice to real charity. Again, a noble ideal had been perverted.

And now nature itself was crying out against another perversion. The land had been profaned. Human beings, who self-righteously understood themselves to have been given dominion over the earth, had exploited God's diverse creation to the point of extinction.

Gurion thought that maybe now he understood God's true calls to chivalry and charity and how those calls had been corrupted. But he did not understand dominion's true call. Kneeling before the ancient oak, all he could see was the disastrous consequences of a confused generation.

Lost in his thoughts, he did not hear Dorothy's approach.

"I thought you had gone back," she said softly.

Gurion was startled by her voice and then relieved. "Dorothy! I was worried about you. These robes—the people of the village are infuriated by them. They threw stones at me. I thought that you . . . I'm so glad you're all right."

The first glow of morning brightened the sky. The people of the village would be up soon. The people who threw stones would be gathering.

"I failed." Dorothy sat dejectedly at the foot of the tree. "I came to the weeping oak to find out more about Cara's world, to discover what went wrong, but all I found was pain."

"Cara's world is gone," Gurion said. "Even in Cara's time, nature had ended. She found solace in the branches of this tree. It was as close as she could get to the land. But one lone tree in a village filled with contempt for nature? . . . There was no hope for Cara."

"No, you are wrong. Cara found more here than you know. This tree has been here for hundreds of years, witnessing the passing of time. History is recorded in its sapwood."

Gurion looked doubtful, but Dorothy continued boldly.

"I cleaned the old sap from its trunk. Every time I touched its dried sap, I saw pictures of what had happened to the land. Mostly the pictures that I saw, or felt, were pictures of sorrow and pain. Something terrible happened here, Gurion. The closer I got to the living sap, the stronger the images were. But I was afraid to see the whole vision. I was afraid to release the living sap. There is a sickness in the land, and somehow we are a part of it."

There was a long silence. The morning sun made its way above the eastern hills. The people who jeered at Dorothy, who laughed at Gurion's pain, would be coming soon.

Gurion's gray world of shadows began to take on the colors of day. He saw that the area surrounding the oak had been groomed with meticulous care. A small mound, under cover of the tree's crown of branches, was outlined with smooth stones. He wondered who had taken such good care of Cara's grave, and then remembered Dorothy.

"You fixed up the grave nicely." He had been so preoccupied with his fears about the land, his guilt, that he had pushed Cara's story out of his mind. But seeing Dorothy's yellow robe brought back a flood of memories.

"I think she saw the whole vision," Dorothy said. "She almost lived in the oak tree's branches. She must have cleaned away the old sap, like I did. She would have known about the pictures, the images."

"She loved this old tree," Gurion said. "She would have wanted to know everything about it. But after her fever, after she lost her hearing and her speech—"

"No one would have listened to her anyway. Even if she could have told them, they wouldn't have listened." Dorothy turned away from Gurion and faced the rising sun.

"Maybe the important thing is that *she* listened." Gurion walked to Cara's grave and touched the flat rock Dorothy had placed as a headstone. "It changed her and gave her strength. She knew her place in the land."

Dorothy looked back at Gurion and smiled. "Yes, that's what I felt when I saw the images, when I had my vision. I felt I was related to the land. I know it sounds crazy, but I sensed that the tree was my cousin, that we shared the same destiny."

"Perhaps we do." Gurion was not smiling. "When the town wakes up, we are going to be targets for their anger. There is something about the community of hope that they despise."

"Yes, I know. They didn't do me any physical harm yesterday, but there are bound to be some in the crowd today who want to get rid of us any way they can. And they know where to find us. They know we are here because of the tree. Perhaps we should leave. There's nothing we can do here to change what has happened."

"I think the tree is our only way back to the Hall of Service," Gurion said. He saw the surprise on Dorothy's face.

"But I thought you said it was the mountain," she replied.

"I know that's what I said, but I was wrong." Gurion paused. "After you left the community of hope I followed the trail all the way to the mountaintop. There was nothing there. At every step I felt myself being drawn in the opposite direction—down here to the tree."

"But how are we supposed to get from the tree to the Hall of Service?" Dorothy asked.

"I don't know. We can't follow its roots back in time—"

"That's it! Don't you see? We *can* follow its roots!"

"I don't understand," Gurion said.

"The sap! The living sap! I was nearly carried back in time just by touching the dried layers. I saw images and pictures that belonged to a time long ago. The eyes are still crusted with a solid resin. When I got to the eyes, I was overwhelmed."

Gurion could hear the sounds of people approaching. A few angry voices shouted words to ignite the crowd. Fear paralyzed him. This was a lynch mob coming, and he and Dorothy were to be the victims.

"Well, if you have any ideas you better move fast!"

Dorothy faced the tree and reached hesitantly toward the solid mass of dried sap that filled the hollow sockets high up on the trunk. The aura of grief radiating from the yellow resin burned her fingers. She pulled back.

By now the crowd was visible, moving up the street toward them. Gurion saw Dorothy pull back a second time in pain. She was grappling with a future and a past that were not her own, that were beyond her understanding.

"Hold on to my robe!" he shouted to her in desperation. Then he clawed at the dried sap with both hands.

His fingers pierced the tree's armor of pain. Like eyes, his fingers led his consciousness into the living heart of the tree. The sap overwhelmed him and swallowed him up. Everywhere there was pain, but somehow he was shielded from it. He saw the pain of the earth, and understood it, but was not destroyed by it.

Soon he felt himself rooted in the land. He was earth-kin. He understood the land from the point of view of the ancient oak. He felt the oppression that emanated from the crowd in the same way the land felt their oppression. He stood helpless against the poison they exhaled. He sensed the earth shriveling and dying around him.

In his vision he was completely at the mercy of the crowd. He was nothing in their sight. They could do whatever they wanted to him, and he could do nothing to stop them. They attacked him, and he saw that they were attacking themselves, but he could not warn them. Their eyes glowed like false gods. They worshiped their pompous achievements, their own mean deeds. But their color was fading with the land, from green to sickly yellow.

Then his vision changed. He saw not what was but what

could be. The crowd was transformed. Instead of greed and egoism feeding a sick and perverted dominion, a dominion characterized by selfish possession and exploitation, Gurion saw the possibility of a different kind of dominion of the earth, a dominion of love.

The people thus transformed viewed him and the land with respect and honor. They saw an intrinsic value there which they had no right to exploit, because the land did not belong to them. They understood that the responsibility to care for the land rested in them. They were its stewards serving the One to whom the land belonged. They served the land with love because they loved the One who had created it and offered it to them for their judicious use.

Gurion felt nature being honored. Instead of an overwhelming pain, he felt overwhelming respect. And with that respect came healing. The people-transformed became earth-kin with him. They were given the gift of being able to see into the hearts of plants and animals. The sickly yellow of the land changed in hue to the brilliant green of hope.

Suddenly Gurion understood the call to dominion in a new light. He saw that stewardship of the land was an essential part of the call to service. Dominion was not a license to exploit the earth's natural resources; it was, rather, a sacred office that humanity had betrayed.

The earth had been handed over to human beings in trust. Chosen to be stewards of creation, we were called to be fair and just in *all* our relationships—not only person-to-person but person-to-earth as well.

Then, as quickly as it had come, the vision was gone.

Gurion felt himself suspended in a blackness that was as thick and sticky as sap. All his senses were jammed simultaneously by an interference that numbed him like death itself. He felt completely disconnected from time and space.

He screamed into the silence, and the silence was not disturbed.

Gurion sat up abruptly, startled by the sound of his own scream. The smell of damp earth told him he was underground. He tried to move, but something held tight to his robe. He couldn't make it out at first, but when his eyes adjusted to the darkness he saw that it was Dorothy.

He tried to wake her, but she did not respond. She would not release her grip. For a moment he was afraid she was dead. But then he saw that she was breathing.

His hands were sticky with sap. He rubbed them in the dirt to try to clean them, but the sap clung to him like guilt.

Like the tree and the land he had come from, he felt wounded. He needed time for healing. And Dorothy was probably more wounded than he. Her breathing was not as deep now, and she was beginning to stir. He decided not to hurry her but to give her time to revive at her own pace.

A dark figure emerged through a shaft of daylight and moved quickly down the tunnel toward Gurion and Dorothy. Gurion faced the approaching shape, too tired to be afraid.

"We'd better get her somewhere more comfortable." It was Kendra. "You both look as if you need a little attention."

Kendra hefted Dorothy onto her back and moved quickly toward the shaft of sunlight. Gurion followed. All at once he was overcome by fatigue. He plodded heavily toward the tunnel's opening, trying to keep pace with Kendra.

The chatter of squirrels scolded him as he emerged from the tunnel. Birds fluttered and chirped in the branches above him. The bright yellow of Dorothy's robe shone boldly against the green landscape of the island. Gurion felt pale by contrast. He had been too long in a dying land.

I wrote for this reason: to test you and to know whether you are obedient in everything.

—2 Cor. 2:9

5

OBEDIENCE

"Will you be leading us to the Hall of Service again?" Dorothy asked Kendra, after she and Gurion had rested and eaten. Kendra had brought them, confused and broken, into the warmth and security of her hearth and sung them back to health.

"All in good time, my child. But for now there is enough to learn right here on the island." Kendra smiled. "It is my responsibility to care for you while you are in my keeping."

"The place we came from . . . there was so much grief, so much pain. It all seemed so hopeless."

Dorothy took a deep breath to try to compose herself. The land of the weeping oak had taken its toll on her and Gurion. When Kendra had found them they were weak and deeply scarred. But the soothing music of her healing song had restored a measure of their vigor.

"There are no futures set in stone, my child. And no sorrows that have not already been redeemed." Kendra's voice was firm but kind. "If you don't like the future you visited, make it a different one."

"We can do that?"

"Every act has consequences, good and bad. Choose your actions wisely, and with purpose." Kendra was weaving a cloak out of a coarse homespun yarn, blending several shades of blue and gold into an intricate pattern. As she worked her yarn, she hummed softly to herself.

"It doesn't seem possible that our actions would really make that much difference." This time it was Gurion who spoke. The experience in the dying land had left him skeptical.

"Why do you say that?" Kendra asked him.

"Because we don't have any power. No one cares what we think. No one listens to what we say."

Kendra paused to consider Gurion's objection. "Power is a word that is greatly misunderstood."

"In my world, power is a commodity of lords and of those in the favor of lords. It comes with wealth and strength and position," Dorothy observed. "There's nothing very difficult to understand about it."

"So it would seem," Kendra mused.

"We don't have lords anymore. But it's still the people with money who seem to have all the power," Gurion said. He could see Kendra was not convinced. Nothing was simple with her.

Kendra shook her head. "Money has the power to

intimidate. It can buy position and strength of arms, but none of these are the power ordained."

With that, Kendra excused herself and left them alone.

In the week that Gurion had spent on the island, a week that did not exist for Dorothy—who had been inside the timeless Hall of Service—he had learned to respect Kendra greatly. She had helped him understand his experience with chivalry without ever really talking to him directly about it. Somehow she found ways to let him discover things on his own.

He knew she would find some unexpected and unorthodox way to lead them to a new understanding of the kind of power they might hold to change the world. She had said their actions might have consequences powerful enough to make a different future. He felt Dorothy's resistance, and his own, to what she was saying. But Kendra respected that resistance. It was not a barrier to her.

Gurion nearly opened his mouth to try to explain all this to Dorothy. Then he stopped. It was best for her to discover it for herself.

"Come on, let's explore the island." He could see that Dorothy was not too excited by the idea. "There are legends and stories about giant flying dragons and all kinds of wizardry."

"I don't believe in dragons and wizards," she replied.

"Well, then, you have nothing to fear. Maybe we can find out how all the stories got started in the first place."

The island was still covered, as it was every day, by the mysterious morning mist. It took Gurion awhile to get his bearings. Kendra had taken them to a cave on the north side of the island, near the tunnel where she had found them. Gurion knew the south perimeter of the island and the main trail leading into the island's interior. He had spent a week with Kendra in the center of the island, near the enchanted arena filled with the specters of knights and dragons. But he had never been on the island's north shore.

From the entrance to their cave, trails led in three directions. One trail led east, back toward the tunnel where Kendra had found them. Another trail led south, into the interior of the island and, no doubt, toward the large clearing where the arena was located. The third trail led west, along the north shore of the island.

Gurion chose the trail west, to the part of the island he had not yet explored. Kendra had told him when he first met her that much of the island was enchanted. He wasn't sure exactly what this meant. But he remembered the convincing images that filled the arena. He remembered the bent shape that watched him approach the island and stalked him as he made his way to the interior. He remembered the spidery figure that nearly had him in its clutches.

According to Kendra, much of what happened on the island was pure illusion. Perhaps. But Gurion had a hunch that some of it was very real indeed.

Dorothy was captivated by the mysterious impression the island conveyed. Its bent and gnarled trees, its thorny underbrush, its blanket of mist—all this left her with a spooky feeling, even though she didn't believe a word of what Gurion said about dragons and wizards.

There was an air of danger that put her on her guard. She walked cautiously, careful to stay within sight of Gurion, watching for strange or unexpected movements in the mist. She sensed the presence of something beyond her understanding and unconsciously awaited its arrival.

It came suddenly.

A distant whistling sound moved rapidly through the trees in their direction. Moments later a powerful whirlwind took a position immediately in front of them on the path, blocking their way. The column of air rotated violently, a tumultuous rush that left them breathless.

Gurion retreated, walking slowly backward until he nearly collided with Dorothy, who had halted out of respect for the whirling mass of air.

A strangely familiar voice spoke to them from out of the whirlwind. "Servants of the mist, I have chosen you. Will you serve the breath of life?"

Gurion was speechless. All he could do was search Dorothy's face for an answer. After a moment's pause, she replied, "You are the voice that called us here. We are committed unto your service." Gurion swallowed hard, trying to regain his voice, but could manage only a silent nod.

"Go then to the source of the island mist, the bubbling waters of a hot spring in the northwest corner of the island. Three times you will be confronted by false images that will try to lure you off the trail. Pay them no heed. But never forget what you know to be true about service. Be true to your hearts as well as your minds.

"When you find the hot spring, beware of the sulfurous vapors. An old man is the keeper of the mist. You must listen carefully to what he tells you to do and follow his directions precisely.

"You will meet others on the trail who seek the same treasure you have been sent to retrieve. They are bigger and more powerful than you, but do not be discouraged. It is you I have chosen."

With that the whirlwind rose slowly from the ground and then shot into the sky, disappearing through the heavy fog.

Dorothy and Gurion watched the fog above them being swept into ghostly gyrations by the ascending whirlwind. They both felt an eddy stirring within—a soul-swirling dizziness. Mouths open, gaping at what had been revealed to them, they stood silently in awe of what had transpired.

Then, slowly, the realization of what they had been asked to do, the task they had been chosen to perform, began to settle on them, like the damp mist that embraced the island.

"Do you think we can find it?" Dorothy asked.

"It shouldn't be too difficult. We can't be more than an hour or two away from the northwest corner right now." Then his expression changed from cautious confidence to panic. "The treasure! We don't have any idea what we're supposed to retrieve!"

"Maybe the old man will know," Dorothy said hopefully. "Anyway, we can't do anything about that now. We have to trust the voice."

The trail opened itself begrudgingly. Visibility was impeded by the fog, making forward progress, at times, a matter of faith. Gurion's imagination stalked him with images of dragons and spidery creatures lurking everywhere. Even Dorothy found the mist unnerving.

They had walked for less than fifteen minutes when something caught Dorothy's attention. She stopped and listened with her whole being.

"What's the matter?" Gurion asked.

"Shhh! I heard something."

Gurion strained to detect any kind of unusual sound, but he heard nothing. "It's probably just your imagination."

"No. Someone cried for help. I'm sure of it."

Both Dorothy and Gurion leaned into the silence and waited.

"Please help me!" The voice was so faint it was barely distinguishable.

"Did you hear that? It sounded like a child."

"Yes. It came from over there." Gurion pointed off the trail to the south. "It couldn't be very far."

"Come on! Hurry!" Dorothy pushed her way through the thorny brush and disappeared.

Gurion started to follow and then remembered the voice's warning about false images trying to lure them off the trail. The voice had said to pay them no heed. Was this distressed child more of the island's enchantment? Was the emergency nothing more than an illusion to test their obedience to the voice?

"Help me! Please help!" the child cried out again, louder than before.

"Gurion, where are you? Come quickly." Dorothy's call was no illusion.

Gurion rushed blindly into the underbrush where Dorothy had disappeared. Within a minute or two he found himself in a small clearing. Dorothy was kneeling over a little girl who looked frightened and hungry but otherwise unharmed.

"Help me get her back to the cave," Dorothy said. "Kendra will know what to do."

But the child had no intention of going anywhere. She clung to the trunk of a small tree as if her life depended on it. And no matter how hard Dorothy and Gurion coaxed, they couldn't get the little girl to agree to go with them.

"What are we going to do?" Gurion asked, after nearly an hour had passed and it became obvious the child wasn't going to budge. "We're supposed to be on our way to the hot spring."

"Can't you see how upset this child is?" Dorothy scolded. "The hot spring will have to wait. We can't leave her here alone like this."

Then, from out of nowhere, Kendra appeared. She touched the child's cheek and the young girl stopped crying. "It was noble of you to come to the little one's defense, but you must return to the trail now and continue on your quest."

Gurion thought he saw Kendra smile. But before he had a chance to speak, she took the child softly in her arms and hurried away without another word.

Back on the trail, Gurion shared his concerns with

Dorothy. "What if the child was there to lure us off the path? We did not obey the voice. You said it yourself; we're committed to the service of the voice. I think that must mean we're supposed to obey the voice no matter what. If that was some kind of test back there, we must have failed it."

By now Dorothy and Gurion were getting hungry. It was nearly noon and the mist was beginning to burn off. When they had left the cave in the morning, they had no idea they would be involved in a quest. They were unprepared.

"How much farther to the hot spring?" Dorothy asked.

"I don't think it could be more than an hour from here, but I don't really know for sure."

Gurion sensed Dorothy's unspoken question. The only trees with edible fruit he had seen were crab apples. And it was hours since he had seen even one of these.

But fortune was smiling on them. Around the next turn stood a lone tree with about half a dozen crab apples. Gurion picked the fruit and gave half to Dorothy. Then they looked for a place to sit down and eat.

In their hurry to get the little apples they had not noticed an old man, sitting silently by the side of the road. Gurion was a little startled by his sudden appearance. But Dorothy greeted him politely.

"Hello! We didn't see you sitting there. Are you all right?"

The old man was slow to respond. He seemed to be having a little trouble breathing.

"I was just trying to get up the energy to pick those apples myself. It's a long way to the next tree."

Gurion looked at Dorothy. Then he spoke. "We have more here than we need. May we share with you?" Gurion offered the old man one of his three small apples, and Dorothy did the same.

The old man ate the two apples with such relish that Dorothy and Gurion were astonished. It appeared that he had not eaten for quite some time.

"I'm really not very hungry, and I don't care much for crab apples anyway," Gurion said. "Would you like the other two?" He held out what remained of his skimpy lunch to the old man, who hesitated for only a moment before devouring the wild fruit.

Dorothy looked longingly at the two small morsels she held in her hand. She was hungry, but she saw the old man's need. She polished them against her robe and presented them to him. After he had finished eating he spoke.

"You are not the first to pass this way. Two hunters were here earlier. They stripped the tree of all but a few apples and didn't give me even a passing glance. I'm afraid I wandered too far from my cabin this morning and now I don't have the strength to get back. If you will only help me make it home, I will gladly share a lunch with you."

"Of course we'll help you!" Dorothy could see Gurion's anxiety as she offered their assistance. She knew he was concerned about the quest and about the warning not to be lured from the trail. But this detour, like the earlier one, could not be avoided. The old man needed their help.

With some difficulty, the two of them got the old man to his feet. He walked between them, leaning heavily on their shoulders for support. Little by little they made their way through the bent trees, following a path that was barely wide enough for one. Finally, they reached a small cabin and helped the old man up the steps into his kitchen.

They had no sooner entered the cabin when the old man's color improved and his energy returned. He sat his visitors down at the table and prepared them a hot lunch that was as delicious as anything they had ever tasted.

It was midafternoon before they found themselves back on the main trail to the hot spring.

"I'm afraid we are not very good when it comes to following instructions," Gurion said to Dorothy as they walked. "Twice we have disobeyed the warning of the voice and allowed ourselves to be lured off the trail. Sure, we can justify our actions with the best of intentions, but the fact remains: We have failed to obey."

Dorothy could see how discouraged and disappointed Gurion was in himself.

"I suppose we could have ignored the old man and left him by the trail to starve," she chided. "Or we could have tossed him an apple, like alms to a beggar, and gone on our merry way."

"I didn't mean that!" Gurion's voice broke as he choked back his emotion. "You know what I meant! Don't you take any of this seriously? We're here for one reason and one reason only—to serve the voice. There's got to be some important reason why we were called. Maybe it's more important than a lost child or a tired, hungry old man. Maybe we are not making the right choices!"

Dorothy softened her resistance to Gurion's fear. "I think we are doing the best we can. Maybe we are making mistakes, but they are honest ones. It does bother me that we have been lured from the trail. I was there too when the voice spoke to us; I know what was said. But the voice also told us to be true to our hearts. Somehow I think that is more important than blind obedience."

"I hope you're right. But from now on I'm going to do everything in my power to stay on this trail, no matter what!" Gurion was adamant.

Dorothy was trying to think of a way to reply when she noticed smoke on the trail in front of them. "Gurion! There's a fire up there!"

They rushed ahead to discover a small brush fire beginning to burn out of control. They stamped frantically at the leading edge of the fire until they had it contained in a small rectangle. It took nearly all the energy they had. When the fire was finally out they discovered an abandoned campfire. Nearby was evidence of a recent kill; the remains of a doe littered the ground.

"She was killed with an arrow," Gurion observed. "Apparently, whoever did it carved out one meal and left the rest of the carcass to rot."

Sickened by the senseless and wasteful slaughter of a fellow creature, Dorothy and Gurion felt, again, the pain of the weeping oak. Their own wounds from the dying land were reopened. How could human beings have so little respect for one of God's creatures?

Precious little time was left in the day. Whatever treasure

they had been sent to retrieve was important enough that the voice had appeared to them and enlisted their service. They had to do their very best not to fail. These detours had slowed their progress. There could be no further delay.

But just as they were about to get started again, Gurion's attention was distracted. Dorothy saw him studying the brush just beyond the area burned by the fire.

"What is it, Gurion?"

"I thought I saw something move. It looked like a fawn."

Dorothy strained her eyes to see. The fawn blended into the brush, making it almost impossible to see. If it had been still, neither she nor Gurion would have spotted it. But it was moving. It was trying to stand up, but it could not. Something was wrong.

"It probably belongs to the doe that was killed," Gurion guessed. "And it looks injured."

Dorothy waited silently. She was not about to be the one who insisted on another delay. But Gurion could see the pain in her eyes, and he could feel the pain in his own heart. The memory of the dying land was too fresh. They had been made earth-kin, and this fawn was one of their own.

This time it was Gurion who led them off the trail. Three times they had been lured away from the path. Three times they had disobeyed the voice's warning.

A stray arrow had penetrated the fawn's flank. It had lost quite a bit of blood. Gurion removed the arrow and tore strips from his shirt to make a bandage.

"I don't think the arrow did any serious damage," Dorothy said hopefully. "But someone is going to have to take care of her. She can't survive on her own."

"Let's take her to the old man and see if he can be responsible for her," Gurion said.

Dorothy looked at him with tears of appreciation. She knew how much he wanted to continue on the quest, how important it was to him to be obedient to the voice. But the fawn, like the child and the old man, could not be ignored.

As human beings, they were rooted in the land. They had been chosen in an age beyond memory, beyond time itself, to be God's stewards, caretakers. The land was in their care. They had a moral responsibility toward it that cried out for obedience with as much legitimacy as the law itself. It wasn't enough to be ethical in their relationships with God and other people. The land insisted on an ethical relationship as well.

The old man welcomed them and took the fawn into his cabin. "She is going to be all right," he promised. "I'll take good care of her."

Before they left he prepared a knapsack full of food for them. It would soon be dinnertime, but somehow he knew they could not possibly stay. The voice called them with an urgency even the old man could feel.

With renewed energy they moved swiftly down the trail. The sun was low in the sky when the sound of running water caught their attention. As they approached the bubbling waters of the hot spring, a husky voice took them by surprise.

"Well, what have we here? If it isn't a couple of fellow prospectors!"

Dorothy and Gurion turned to see two well-outfitted men sitting in the cover of a large tree. The men were powerfully built. They radiated a self-assurance that was intimidating. One had a dark complexion, the other was fair-skinned.

The fair-skinned warrior demanded, "What brings you to the isle of mist?"

He was looking straight at Gurion when he spoke, but it was Dorothy who answered. "We were told we would meet you here. We have come for directions from the keeper of the mist."

"Well, what took you so long?" the man with the dark complexion taunted. "We've been here for hours. But then, we did not stray from the trail." Both men had a hearty laugh at the expense of the young newcomers. "We watched as you were lured away by the child. The instructions were not to leave the trail. But then, that's the trouble with your generation. You're hard of listening!" Again there was hearty laughter.

"And let me guess," the fair-skinned one added. "You let the old beggar lead you off the trail as well." The expression on Gurion's face started them laughing again. "Shame, shame. This quest is not for the weakhearted. You may as well—" But the appearance of an old man silenced him in midsentence. It was the same old man that Gurion and Dorothy had befriended.

"Don't let me interrupt your fun," the old man said. "What was it you were about to say? They may as well go home? No, I don't think so. They have come here without once straying from the way."

"But how can that be?" Gurion asked timidly. "He is right. We were lured from the trail three times. And each time we knew in our hearts that we were disobeying the warning of the voice."

"Did you indeed?" The old man could hardly keep from smiling. "Do you think the voice referred to the physical path itself when you were warned not to be lured from the trail by false images? Of what possible importance is the physical path? The voice spoke of the trail of the true service. You were tempted three times to deny the true service—"

"What are you talking about, old man?" The man with the dark complexion interrupted. "We followed our instructions to the letter. The voice said to stay on the trail. We stayed on the trail. Don't give us any nonsense about some symbolic trail of service. We were obedient to the letter of the law!"

"Yes, but not to the spirit." The old man's voice was gentle yet firm. "You forgot what you knew to be true about service. You did not follow your hearts."

There was some grumbling, but the old man—continued speaking to Dorothy and Gurion. "You, my friends, were true to your hearts. When you took time away from the quest to come to the service of a lost child, you demonstrated what chivalry really means—for chivalry is not as much about honor as it is about solidarity with the weak and defenseless.

"You demonstrated what charity really means when you respected the beggar by the side of the road as a whole person, instead of merely throwing alms his way. You could have just given him an apple and gone on your way. But you took time to listen to his story. You involved yourselves in his problems, his life. You allowed him to share his own gifts with you.

"When you remembered your responsibility to the land, you demonstrated what dominion really means. You did not treat the land as if it were yours to exploit and plunder. Instead, you gave yourselves up in service to the land. You acted as faithful stewards. You did not inflict pain on the land, but instead you felt its pain as earth-kin. You bound up its wounds.

"But that is not all. In everything you did, through chivalry, charity, and dominion, you demonstrated what obedience really means. You were true to your hearts, true to yourselves, even when you thought it meant you were failing.

"The voice is proud of you. In discovering what obedience really means, you have likewise discovered the key to understanding the power ordained—the power to change the world. And that power, my friends, is the treasure you have come to retrieve."

The words fell heavily on Gurion and Dorothy. Everything they knew about power frightened them, repulsed them.

The old man began to walk toward the hot bubbling waters of the spring. The sun had set, and the air was cool enough to change the warm moisture from the spring to clouds of ethereal mist.

"Come, my friends. The time has come to give you the directions you will need to retrieve the power ordained."

Gurion and Dorothy followed.

6

POWER

The keeper of the mist stood knee deep in the waters of the bubbling pool. He raised his arms to the sky. Clouds of white vapor began to gather on the waters and drift toward the heavens. Within minutes, Gurion and Dorothy were smothered in fog.

"Behold! You are witness to the secret source of the mist."

The island's mysteries had lain hidden in the cloudy cover for centuries. Few had ventured to explore its harsh landscape. But if the island was covered in a cloak of mist, it was also shrouded in legend. Stories had been passed from generation to generation: tales bizarre and full of wonder, fables filled with a heart-stopping power.

No one knew for sure how much fact there was in any of the stories. No one questioned the depth of truth they all contained.

The island was a world of hidden shadows, shades of reality too frightening to face in full daylight. Because of its screen of secrecy it had come to symbolize the realm of fears hidden deep in the unconscious island of the mind. That was, perhaps, part of the power of its mystery. It was a mirror into the dark secrets each of us hides within. Few souls were brave enough to seek the answers that might be hidden there.

And now Dorothy and Gurion stood at the very center of the island's unknown and unfathomable power. Up until now they had been little more than outsiders, protected by the mist's veil. Once inside the mist, they had to be ready to face their own fears.

The keeper of the mist called them into the water. "Come, my friends. Kick off your boots and feel the heat of the earth." They waded cautiously into the vaporous pool. Its waters were nearly too hot to endure. It smelled of sulfur.

Only a faint afterglow of the day's dying light charged the fog and made it vaguely luminous. Evening was giving way to the night's darkness.

Gurion felt himself relaxing, surrendering to the dreamy landscape and the steamy vapors. He heard the old man talking to Dorothy, warning her not to breathe too deeply. But his voice sounded far away.

Images began to rise from the water. Bent shapes stalked him. Shadows of the island watched him secretly from behind gnarled trees. Out of the dreamworld images of underbrush crawled, once again, the large spidery figure that had paralyzed him with fear.

In his dream, Gurion saw the black hooded tunic that bore the symbol of a red hourglass, the symbol of poison and dread. He saw that the hood was empty of anything but shadows, and out of its emptiness yellow eyes shined.

"What are you doing on my island?" The question hung in the air.

Gurion felt himself being lifted by crooked appendages. Arms and legs wrapped around him until he was incapable of moving. He felt himself being carried away, through the mist, through the underbrush, and down into the earth.

A fire burned in the depths of the earth, a fire so hot it consumed the very rock that contained it. The glow of the lava lit the large underground cavern with an eerie red light. Gurion was carried into the hellish cavern. The powerful arms of his predator released him and left him helpless on the floor of the large room.

Gurion felt the sting of poison numbing his senses. He could see everything that was going on around him, but he was powerless to move. He tried to cry out for help, but the paralysis even affected his vocal cords.

In the dim light he saw the cavern crawling with activity. He heard the clank of chains. Hundreds of shapes moved about in a forced rhythm. They were carrying loads, heavy bags filled with rock from deep within the earth. It appeared to be some sort of mining operation. But the miners were prisoners, enslaved by the same force that had brought Gurion into their midst.

The bags of rock were fed into the pool of magma, like logs added to a fire. Every bag ignited with a rage of fumes and thunder. And the lava reddened its glare to a new intensity. The power of the lava was approaching explosive levels. Still the endless line of rock carriers dumped their cargo into the fiery pool.

Out of the corner of his eye Gurion could see the spidery figure returning. Again he felt himself snarled by arms and legs and carried away, to a room still deeper in the earth—deeper in the unconscious region of his mind.

He dreamed a nightmare of power.

The forces of good had organized themselves into a mighty army. For too long evil had raised its ugly head. The time had come to wipe it out entirely, to rid the world of evil's curse.

It would not be an easy task. Evil's troops were legion. Though the forces of good were confident of victory, it was a victory that would not come cheaply. Tens of thousands would die fighting for the right that would ultimately prevail. Even before the battle began there was mourning. It was a terrible price to pay, but it could not be avoided.

There were those weaklings who resisted the holy war. Voices had been raised opposing the whole idea, pleading for a negotiated settlement. As if one could strike a bargain with the devil. But the stronger voices had won out. Right was right. There could be no compromising.

Two mighty armies tested each other's nerve. The evil army had weapons so horrible and inhuman that just the thought of them led to despair. Only minds perverted by evil could even dream of such weapons.

Protective gear had been issued. Every possible precaution had been taken against the use of evil's weapons. But the forces of good would not be overpowered or intimidated by threats. They had weapons of their own even more horrible. If the evil army wanted to boast weapons of mass destruction, let them take notice. The power of good could be deadly too–perhaps even more deadly.

It had been a long hard struggle for the leaders of the forces of good to organize and outfit their army. Most difficult to overcome was their natural instinct to love. Love had no place on the battlefield. Any fool knew that. It was a weakness that could not be afforded. Until the battle was won, and evil banished forever, love would be replaced by moral determination. In order for good to triumph over evil, its soldiers needed to be powerful and unyielding.

The enemy was full of deceit and treachery. Its leaders would stop at nothing to undermine the confidence of the forces of good, to lead good people astray. But the people of evil were just as susceptible to well-thought-out campaigns of lies and deception. Two could play their evil game.

And so the leaders of the army of the good learned the skills they needed to wage an effective fight against the forces of evil. Morality became their watchword, hatred of evil their battle cry. They forged their troops into well-trained and obedient soldiers who would follow orders unquestioningly. The stage was set, the battle ready to begin.

Unfortunately, the leaders of forces for good, in spite of everything they had done to rally their troops, had been unable to convert a small remnant of their people from the foolishness of love to the power for moral determination.

This remnant held out for love. They dared to speak out against their brothers and sisters who had sacrificed everything—who were willing even to lay down their own lives to defeat the powers of evil once and for all.

Secret meetings took place among the most powerful and influential members of the forces for good. It was decided that this misguided remnant threatened the whole operation. If they were not silenced, they might undermine the determination of the troops. As traitors to the cause, they had aligned themselves with the enemy. The good army had no choice but to insist on their loyalty—on penalty of death.

One by one, the dissenters were brought before a special council and given the opportunity to renounce their traitorous ways and pledge their allegiance to the sovereign forces for good and the power for moral determination. If they refused, they were to be executed as traitors.

The leaders of the good army were a little concerned that the forces of evil might strike before the investigations were complete. They secretly cursed the remnant for standing in their way. But the forces of evil seemed content to allow the good army all the time it needed to purge its ranks of traitors.

Even though the traitorous remnant was a relatively small percentage of the population, their numbers were by no means insignificant. They made no effort to defend themselves through violent means. However, again and again they stated their convictions before the special council. They argued that no earthly power could defeat the forces of evil because power itself was evil too.

Gurion's dream tore him apart. He twisted and turned in agony. He felt the sting of evil. He saw its bent shape, its yellow eyes. He was paralyzed by the poison of its fear. In the good army he saw a chance, at least, for the evil that had paralyzed him to be defeated. He wanted to believe in the power for good. He could see the stakes were high and the cause was just.

He knew that somehow he was tied to the fate of the good army. A real battle was being waged in the deep recesses of his unconscious mind. The veil of mist had been lifted. He could clearly see the forces assembling. He was trapped in a world of shadows, where he faced frightening questions, unspeakable decisions.

The island that had called him had become a mirror of his own mind. Both good and evil were represented there. Volcanic fires of passion burned within him, a passion to serve what was just and right. He wanted to believe in the power for good, but he sensed that something was wrong.

Dorothy's attention was focused purposefully on the keeper of the mist. She could not pull herself away from what he was saying. His words were almost hypnotic in their intensity. He was speaking of power, warning against the lure of its addiction. Then she saw Gurion sinking helplessly, unconsciously, into the sulfurous waters.

"Gurion!" Dorothy moved quickly to his side and kept him from going under. "Help me get him out of here! The vapors have overwhelmed him."

The keeper of the mist lifted Gurion from the water and

carried him away through the fog. He led Dorothy through the underbrush and down into the earth.

A natural furnace glowed in the underground cavern, a living fire of smelted rock. One whole side of the cavern radiated the energy generated from the same lava that heated the waters of the hot spring.

The powerful arms of the keeper of the mist released Gurion and placed him gently on a mattress of straw. "He breathed too deeply of the vapors. There is nothing we can do now but let the nightmare run its course."

"Will he be all right?"

The old man sighed. "It's too early to tell. He is making a dangerous journey without the benefit of the directions he was supposed to receive."

"The directions to retrieve the power ordained?" Dorothy asked.

"Yes. I was instructed by the voice to give precise instructions for you to follow on your journey—"

"But I don't understand. What kind of a journey can he be making? He has lost consciousness."

Gurion was twisting and turning in the straw. Several times he screamed out, but the words were garbled or meaningless. Sweaty tears ran down his face.

The keeper of the mist brought a cloth and a basin of cool water. He sat beside Gurion and wiped the beads of stress and exertion from Gurion's feverish brow.

"Had all gone well, you would be making this journey together. You would have had each other's counsel. As it is, Gurion must rely entirely on his own judgment to—"

"You talk of him as if he were not here," Dorothy interrupted.

"His body is here, but his mind is not," the old man explained. "He is in a dream world dimension."

Dorothy was confused. "But certainly, if he is only dreaming, we have nothing to worry about. Can't you give us the directions we need and send us on our way after he wakes up?"

"I'm afraid that is not possible." He looked tenderly at Dorothy. "The dream *is* the journey. The warm waters and steamy vapors were meant to lead you both into a state of relaxation where, together, you could enter the dimension of the unconscious, the dream world state."

"But what do dreams have to do with retrieving the power ordained?" Dorothy sought desperately for meaning.

"Dreams are far more important than you think. All the decisions, good and ill, that shape our world come first from the dreamworld dimension." The keeper of the mist wrung out the cloth and placed it back on Gurion's forehead.

Timidly Dorothy asked, "Will Gurion have to make decisions that could change the world?"

"The decisions he makes will affect his life . . . and that may change the world. He has been called into the service of the voice. His life is not to be taken lightly—nor is any life."

Dorothy reflected on what the old man had said. She remembered her own dream in the Hall of Service, the dream responsible for leading them into Cara's world.

Gurion's restlessness was getting worse. He threw his arms and legs first to one side and then to the other. He tried to sit up. He called out meaningless strings of words that Dorothy could not understand.

"There must be something we can do!"

"Perhaps . . . there is something." The keeper of the mist studied Dorothy carefully. "Perhaps it is not too late for you to follow. You have shared dreams before. It should not be impossible for you to share this one—even now."

The glow of the lava cast a red shadow on Gurion's face. Dorothy shuddered at the thought of entering Gurion's dream. She looked at him lying helpless on the floor, his face contorted, wrenched into an almost unrecognizable shape. What could he be dreaming? she wondered. What nightmare could have twisted him like this, into the shape of fear?

Gurion watched, paralyzed, as the two mighty armies faced each other on the battlefield. The forces of evil wore mantles of a sickly, sulfurous yellow—the color of poison, of the spider's eyes. It made Gurion feel ill even to look at the evil army. He wanted nothing to do with them. But he had felt their sting. Even as he watched in terror, he felt their dread poison surging through his veins.

The forces of good were dressed in green. But it was not the green of health and life. Somehow it was a shade of green that looked familiar to Gurion. He could look on it with pity but not with hope. It was a wilted, faded green, a dying green. Then he remembered where he had seen it. It was the green of Cara's world, the green of the dying land.

What could this mean? He struggled desperately to understand. He was not thinking clearly. The poison clouded his mind. He fought to believe in the power for good. He strove to see hope represented in the good army. He wanted to be loyal to their cause, to pledge his allegiance and support to the defeat of evil.

But where was the voice in all of this? Through all his struggles in this dreamworld there had been a strange emptiness inside him. He knew he had been called into this world, as he was called in all the others, to serve the voice. Certainly the voice would want him to side with the good enemy. Why was it silent?

Gurion thought of the remnant who had clung to their belief that power was evil. Even now they were being called before the special council to renounce that belief or die. What gave them the strength to stand against the mighty power of the good army?

Something about the courage of this incorrigible remnant gave Gurion a feeling of hope. How could that be? They stood powerless before the forces of good. Judgment had already been pronounced. One by one they were being sentenced to die the death of traitors. Yet Gurion sensed that if hope was to be found in this world, it dwelled in them.

Suddenly Gurion was aware of the presence of the voice.

"I am pleased with you, my child. There is hope yet that the treasure may be retrieved. Remember your quest."

No whirlwind this time, just a flash of recognition, a moment's insight. But it was enough. Gurion could feel his skin begin to tingle. The poison that had numbed and left him paralyzed was beginning to wear off. The power that held him captive was weakening.

Remember your quest. He had been so caught up in the nightmare, in the poison of his own paralyzing fear, that he had forgotten the words that had led him here. For a moment he was lost, marooned on some deserted island of forgetfulness. Then everything started coming back to him.

He had been sent here to retrieve some kind of treasure. That much he could remember. The voice had not said what kind of treasure it was. But he had been warned to beware of the sulfurous vapors. The last thing he could remember, before falling into this dreamworld, was the smell of sulfur.

But there was more. The old man, the keeper of the mist, had said something about the treasure. Gurion struggled to remember just what it was he had said. Something about the treasure being the power ordained—the power to change the world.

Well, Gurion had certainly found all kinds of power represented here. The forces of evil wielded enough power to poison the whole planet. Could it be that the voice wanted him to retrieve *that* power? Perhaps he was to find some way to remove evil's perverted power from them, to call back the threat they embodied. But how could he possibly accomplish such a feat? Even all the forces of good assembled before him might fail at such a task. Surely so monumental a service was not required of him.

The forces of good represented the other great power. They had a much better claim to being the power ordained he had been sent to retrieve. But how could such a power be reclaimed? Could it be called back into a bottle like some genie?

No. In the other worlds Gurion visited, he had not been asked to play savior. He was an observer. It was not his job to step in and solve problems, to wave some kind of wand and make everything okay. In his own world Gurion's actions might make a difference, but here he was powerless to change anything.

How, then, could he retrieve the power ordained? One thing was certain. He could not retrieve it until he discovered what it was. He resolved that as soon as he could move he would walk into the camp of the good army and start asking questions.

The keeper of the mist covered Gurion with a blanket of wool and removed the cloth from his forehead.

"He seems to be sleeping more soundly now. I think it is safe to leave him alone for a while."

Dorothy noticed that a great change had come over Gurion. His fever seemed to have broken and his face looked more relaxed. It appeared that some inner torment had been resolved, as if he had come to a decision.

The old man had patiently explained the process involved in projecting her into Gurion's dream. A series of crucial steps would bring about the desired result—*if* everything went as planned.

First, she needed direct contact with an object that symbolized an experience she and Gurion had shared deeply, an experience that bound them together as a team. She suggested the robes they had been given by the community of hope. But they were back in Kendra's shelter, more than an hour's walk away even in daylight. The keeper of the mist said he could contact Kendra and have her bring the robes. He left the room and returned a few minutes later with news that the robes were on the way.

The next step was to give Dorothy the directions she and Gurion would need in the dreamworld dimension. He warned her again of the lure of power's addiction.

"Do not be fooled by the illusion that problems can be solved by brute force or that good can come of evil."

As Dorothy listened carefully to what the old man was saying, she thought of the way power had been misused by the knights and lords of her own world.

"The power ordained, the power you seek, has nothing to do with intimidation. It is not the power that frightens or threatens. It has nothing to do with weapons. It recognizes neither wealth nor position."

Dorothy wondered what this could be. "How will I recognize this power? It sounds nothing at all like the kinds of power I have experienced."

"When you find the power that empowers the weak, that stands helpless and yet firm against tyranny, that will not intimidate or be intimidated—this is the power you must retrieve."

In the space of time it took for Dorothy's instruction, Kendra had come and gone without so much as a word. Gurion had been helped into his green mantle. Dorothy's yellow robe lay neatly folded beside him. She donned the robe and followed the keeper of the mist to the hot spring.

"Now, chosen one, comes the most delicate step in the

process. You must never lose sight of Gurion in your mind's eye. There is a part of our unconscious mind, our dreaming mind, that connects us with others—especially those with whom we have common ties. You and Gurion have shared dreams before. As you feel yourself relaxing, be mindful of Gurion, and remember your quest."

The old man raised his arms and addressed the voice with the words: "*Ministrare est vivere.*"

The words wove themselves around Dorothy. She could see them dancing in the air. She remembered the ornate arch outside the Hall of Service and the letters carved in stone: MINISTRARE EST VIVERE. All at once she knew what the words meant. She felt herself connected with the mythic pool of humankind's collective knowledge, as if she had stepped into that pool when she entered the waters of the hot spring. *Ministrare est vivere.* To serve is to live. This, then, was the motto of the Hall of Service, the guiding force of all who pledged their lives to the voice's call.

She felt herself floating now above the waters. She could hear the voice of the keeper of the mist, but she could not make out what he was saying. Somehow just the sound of his voice was comforting, reassuring.

She wanted to relax and let herself go entirely, to float carelessly in the soft mist. But then she remembered Gurion and the task that lay before her. She reached down and clung to the yellow fabric of her robe. She pictured Gurion's contorted face, his body lying helpless in the cave. She saw him again, standing before the weeping oak, accepting into himself its pain.

Then she was lost in the mist, swirling in a whirlwind of unconsciousness. She clung blindly to her robe and to the vision of Gurion, past, present, and future.

She dreamed she held a torch of yellow light. She was being chased through a maze of underground tunnels by a silent adversary. She ran into the unknown darkness with nothing but the flame of her torch to light her way, to guide her attempts to escape. She kept looking back over her shoulder to see if she had eluded the enemy who was stalking her. But no matter how fast she ran, no matter how many turns she took to try to lose him, the shadowy figure was always right behind her.

Finally, breathless, she could run no more. She stopped and then collapsed to her knees. When she glanced back, expecting to be overcome by whatever devil it was that pursued her, she saw behind her the shadowy figure kneeling as well. At first she thought it was mocking her. And then she realized that she was being chased by her own shadow.

She was deep in the earth, deep within herself. Dreamworld images spun around her, images from her dreams and the dreams of others. Through her dream she felt connected to all human beings. She sorted through the images that drifted before her, searching for something familiar, something that reminded her of Gurion. But she was lost in a kaleidoscope of the strange and unfamiliar, where a series of constantly changing colors, forms, and events bombarded her until she wanted to scream out in terror.

She felt her hands clenched in fear, grasping something coarse and familiar. Her yellow robe. Yes, finally an image and a color she knew. Yellow robes; she saw an army of yellow robes.

Gurion knew he was dreaming, walking down a grassy hill toward the army that was clad in robes of green. He looked down at himself and discovered that he, too, was dressed in a green robe. He didn't know where the robe had come from. He didn't remember being able to move. But he knew where he was going. He was on his way into the camp of the good army to ask some questions.

In his green robe he would blend in with the troops. He was younger and smaller, but perhaps no one would notice. After all, it was a dream.

Thousands of soldiers were camped on the lowlands. A huge city of tents mushroomed up from the plain. He knew that the forces of evil were camped on the back side of the hill. Each army was waiting for the other to make the first move.

Gurion started thinking about the questions he was going to ask. The more he thought about them, the more hollow they sounded. How could he ask the green army anything? They would think he was a traitor—one of the remnant. They didn't want anyone to question what they were doing.

Anyway, he already knew the answers. He knew how much they wanted to destroy evil. He had felt evil's poison. He wanted it destroyed as much as they did.

But the real question he wanted to ask was about the remnant. What gave them the strength to resist the power of the forces of good? How could they cling to the impossibility of love in the face of the yellow-robed reality camped on the backside of the hill? It was the remnant who held the key to understanding the power ordained. He was certain of it. So why not ask them directly? Yes, of course. That was it. But how would he get to them?

He was nearly down the hill when he was surprised by a half a dozen yellow-cloaked soldiers. They were between him and the camp of the good army. He tried to run, but his fear paralyzed him for an instant, just long enough for them to grab him. They blindfolded and gagged him and tied his hands behind his back. Then they led him back up the hill, a prisoner of the forces of evil.

As they trudged up the hill, Gurion had to remind himself, again, that this was all a dream, a nightmare. He wanted to wake up now. The thought of going into the yellow camp turned his stomach. He knew he was headed in the wrong direction. The answers he needed would not be found in the camp of the evil army. Yet some force was drawing him there.

His captors were trying to decide what to do with him. If they led him into the camp, green-robed, chances are he would be torn limb from limb. But he might be more valuable to them alive. There was no telling what information he could give them with the right kind of encouragement.

They decided to tie him to a tree outside their camp.

One of them would stay behind to guard him while the other five would report to the leaders. But there was bickering over who would remain behind. They all wanted to be present for the commendations that were sure to come for the capture of the first enemy prisoner.

Then a solution presented. What must have been a sentry or lookout emerged from the cover of the underbrush and volunteered to stand guard. Gurion was tied to the nearest tree. He listened despairingly as his captors made their way toward camp.

When they were out of earshot, a familiar voice asked, "Are you all right, Gurion?" The gag and blindfold were removed and Gurion saw the welcome sight of Dorothy's face.

'Tis not the dying for a faith that's so hard, Master Harry–[people] of every nation [have] done that–'tis the living up to it that's difficult.
  –*William Makepeace Thackeray (1811–1863)*, Henry Esmond

7
FAITH

Dreams, even the worst nightmares, are usually predictable. Somewhere deep in the unconscious, the dreamer almost always knows what is about to take place.

That's not to say there are no surprises. Gurion had been surprised by his yellow-cloaked captors, but even their ambush had been predictable. Dorothy's appearance, on the other hand, was an intrusion.

True, her presence was welcome enough. In fact, Gurion couldn't remember a time when he was happier to see anyone. But he had no control over her actions. That was a problem. The dreamer is supposed to control the dream. Unexpected images may appear, but they are the dreamer's images, under the dreamer's control.

But here was Dorothy in her yellow robe.

Up until now it had been Gurion's dream. He knew he

was floundering a bit. He had lost his bearings, at first, and only recently felt himself on track. The treasure he had been sent to retrieve still eluded him. The power ordained was as big a mystery as it had been even before he stepped into the misty waters of the spring.

He had not succeeded in his quest, but neither had he failed. He felt certain that the answers he sought were in the keeping of the remnant—that small vestige of people who refused to see love as a weakness that must temporarily be replaced by power. Faithful to their beliefs, they stood boldly as a surviving memorial to love, even though they were denounced as traitor for doing so. He had only to find a way into their midst.

It was not Dorothy so much as her yellow robe that bothered him. Yellow was the color of evil. It sickened him even to see it. It filled his heart with rage, with hate.

Dorothy understood his uneasiness. He had begun the dream without her. She had invaded the privacy of his personal dreamworld. She was trespassing in his unconscious. But she reminded him that the dream quest had never been his alone. The voice had called them both into this strange world.

She understood, as well, his disgust with her yellow robe. She too had seen visions of the yellow-cloaked army. No one had to tell her what her pale yellow robe symbolized to the forces who opposed them.

But she would not abandon it. Yellow might be the color of evil in this world, but in Cara's world the color of

Dorothy's robe had been a symbol of hope. She believed in that hope, and she would not forsake it no matter what the cost.

And so it was that the colors of evil and good walked arm in arm toward the camp of the green army.

As they made their way back to the lowlands, Dorothy explained what had happened at the hot spring. She did her best to repeat, for Gurion, the instructions that the keeper of the mist had shared with her.

"The treasure we are here to retrieve, the power ordained, is not like any power I know," she confessed, after she had told him all she could remember. "It does not sound like power at all. It sounds almost like foolishness."

"It sounds like the remnant," Gurion muttered.

Now it was Gurion's turn to tell Dorothy about the nightmare of power she had gotten herself into. He told her about the forces of good and the forces of evil. Then he tried to explain the position of the remnant.

"They refuse to support the forces of good. They claim that *all* earthly power is evil."

Gurion was about to continue when Dorothy interrupted him. "If the remnant is right about power itself being evil, it is impossible for the forces of good to win."

"What do you mean?" Gurion asked.

"Whichever side proves to be more powerful will have won a victory for evil."

"I suppose that is what they are saying. But it's even worse than that. The good army is executing them as traitors for refusing to pledge allegiance to the cause."

"But why?" Dorothy protested. "Certainly they are no threat to the forces of good."

"The leaders of the good army are afraid that the remnant's message of love may undermine the troops," Gurion explained. "The good army's vision of a world purged of evil demands some sacrifices. They have no tolerance for moral weakness of any kind—and they see love as weakness."

"But that is insane!" Dorothy insisted. "How can goodness or morality have any meaning without love?"

"I don't know, exactly. But I understand the position of the good army. Evil has got to be eliminated. It is choking the very life out of this world." Gurion felt his own rage erupting within. He, too, hated evil and wanted it destroyed at any cost.

When the camp of the green army was in view, Gurion and Dorothy sat down and considered their options.

"You know that you can't just walk into their camp wearing your yellow robe," Gurion reminded Dorothy. "They will arrest you and probably execute you without even bothering to hear your story. And even if they heard your story, they wouldn't believe it. I don't even believe it myself."

"Well, I'm not removing this robe no matter what happens," Dorothy said. "It means too much to me. I can't change who I am just to please them. My robe represents hope and charity. As far as I can tell, this green army of yours could stand a large dose of both. I will not be intimidated by their threats."

"Well, if you won't take off the robe, will you at least

pretend to be my prisoner?" Gurion pleaded. "Otherwise, both of us will be arrested. We're not going to learn anything that way."

"I'm not going to pretend anything," Dorothy said sharply. "I'm going to stand up for what I believe in; it's as simple as that. The color of this robe does not make me evil. If the green army can't see past the color of my robe, they have no more claim to goodness than the forces of evil."

"You're not being fair to them, Dorothy. Their intentions are good. They are so determined to overcome evil that maybe they have gone a little overboard. But that doesn't make them evil."

"Doesn't it? They may be wearing their precious green, but it seems to me that they are the ones who have taken on the cloak of evil, not me." There was fire in Dorothy's eyes.

"Then what do you suggest we do?" Gurion asked.

"I don't have any plan—except to be faithful to who we are and what we believe. There has to be a certain strength in that kind of honesty."

Gurion knew that Dorothy was in no mood to compromise when it came to her yellow robe. He also knew that the robe was going to get them into trouble. Surely Dorothy could see that too. But if she was willing to risk arrest and possible execution in an attempt to live up to what the robe stood for to her, who was he to insist otherwise?

Anyway, it wouldn't do any good. He knew Dorothy well enough by now to be sure of that. She would do what she thought was right, regardless of the cost.

Gurion spoke softly, almost to himself. "Somehow one of us must get to the remnant. The success of our quest depends on it. If anyone understands about the power ordained in this world, it has to be them. You follow your instincts, and I will follow mine."

Dorothy wasn't exactly sure what they had decided. But she knew there was nothing more to be said. The camp of the green army was less than half an hour's walk away. It was time to see what their true colors really were.

Dorothy had taken only a few steps toward the camp of the green army when she was surrounded by a band of sentinels.

"And where do you think you are going, evil one?" The voice that addressed Dorothy was gruff and firm. Then the leader of the sentinels turned to face Gurion. "And you . . . aren't you a little young to be out taking prisoners?"

Some of the guards laughed nervously. It was clear they were puzzled by these two youngsters robed in yellow and green.

Gurion looked at Dorothy, completely at the mercy of the powerful guards. There was no hope for her. The yellow robe was enough to condemn her. Gurion was tempted for a moment to deny their friendship. He considered pretending he didn't know her, that he had never known her. It would be so easy to say that she was, indeed, his prisoner.

But there was something in the way she refused to be bullied by the sentinels that gave Gurion the courage to stand up for her.

"She is not my prisoner," he said. "She is my friend."

Gurion heard the guards gasp and mutter something about treason, but he was not daunted. "And she is not evil. Can't you see that her robe is not the yellow of evil? It is the color of hope!"

Even as Gurion said the words, he knew they would not be believed. He had to think quickly now, or all would be lost. What could he say that would give them a chance to meet with the remnant?

"Who are you, young man?" The leader of the sentinels asked, almost tenderly. "Do you realize what you are saying? Siding with evil is punishable by death."

"My name is Gurion. And I do not side with evil. I hate it as much as you do. But I happen to believe that *all* earthly power is evil." He looked at Dorothy. "And so does she."

Dorothy had already been bound and gagged. These guards were taking no chances. They were probably afraid she would say something evil, something they were not allowed to hear.

Gurion waited to see if they had taken his bait. If they believed he was one of the remnant, there was a chance he would be imprisoned with them. If he could make them believe that Dorothy, despite her robe, was in the remnant's number—who knows, maybe she would be held there too, at least temporarily.

The guards huddled together and discussed what they should do. Who else but the remnant would be crazy enough to pull such a stunt? But the yellow robe? That was radical even for the remnant.

Finally, the leader of the sentinels threw his arms in the

air in frustration. "I say we turn them both over to the forces guarding the remnant and let *them* decide what to do."

Dorothy and Gurion were marched into the camp. From their position in the middle of the sentinels they were nearly invisible. Gurion thought to himself that he couldn't have hoped for a better cover.

The area holding the remnant was surrounded by barbed-wire fences and guarded heavily on all sides. But within the complex there was relative freedom to move about. The remnant's belief in nonviolence, their denial of power, removed any threat of an organized revolt. The threat they represented was ideological. If the troops were exposed to their ideas about love and the evil of all earthly power, patriotism to the cause might be in jeopardy.

Patriotism was the glue that held the good army together. In order for evil to be defeated, it was absolutely essential that every soldier be faithful to the green banner that flew proudly over the camp.

The leaders of the good army knew that certain compromises had been made with respect to the good that the banner symbolized. Those compromises were unavoidable. The war against the forces of evil could not be won unless the good army learned all the terrible skills it needed to wage an effective fight.

To them, the ends justified the means. It was the good they were fighting for that really mattered, not the road they traveled to get there.

The last thing the leaders of the good army wanted was for the remnant to preach love and nonviolence. In a very real sense the remnant was an even greater threat to the good army than the forces of evil. The evil army could be defeated by the immense power assembled by the forces of good. It would be a costly battle, but the leaders were confident of victory.

If, however, the troops started hearing the remnant's nonsense about love and nonviolence, there was no telling what might happen. Certainly patriotism would be eroded. The concessions that had been made to the very principles they were fighting for were sure to be misunderstood.

One could not fight a war on principles, even the loftiest and best of principles. Principles were useful for boosting patriotic feelings. It was nice to be fighting on the side of good, against the forces of evil. But the reality of war was that it was fought with weapons of power. The most powerful army would prevail. Victory had nothing to do with principles; it had everything to do with power.

Loyalty to the cause, unthinking and unquestioning loyalty, was essential. Without patriotism, without absolute faithfulness to the cause, the power that had been assembled would begin to break down. Too much had been invested in this effort to allow that to happen. Faithfulness to the cause would ensure a victory over the forces of evil. After that victory had been won, love and nonviolence would be luxuries that could be afforded again.

The remnant's message had proved to be an even greater problem than the leaders of the good army had at first anticipated. Some of the guards inside the complex had been converted. These guards had renounced the cause and spread the message of the remnant outside the barbed-wire fence that contained it.

The decision had been made to dispense with all guards inside the complex. And those who guarded the fences were equipped with earplugs and warned against listening to anything the remnant had to say.

New prisoners were treated well by the remnant, even prisoners wearing yellow robes. Dorothy's gag and the ropes that bound her hands were gently removed. A healing lotion was applied to her wrists where the rough fibers had rubbed them raw. Food and drink were offered and gratefully accepted.

Gurion and Dorothy had hardly had time to eat when they were approached by a young woman. She whispered something in Dorothy's ear and then vanished as suddenly as she had appeared. Gurion could see that Dorothy was upset by whatever it was the young woman said.

"What is it, Dorothy?" he asked in a low voice. "What did she say to you?"

"The leaders of the green army have demanded that the remnant turn me over to them immediately."

Gurion was speechless.

"Perhaps we should split up," Dorothy suggested. "If I am captured by the green army, it would be better if you were somewhere safe."

"Sure. I'm going to hide somewhere and let the green army come and get you. What kind of a friend do you think I am?" Gurion had found his voice. "Whatever happens, we're in this nightmare together."

For the remainder of the evening, both Dorothy and Gurion watched nervously for any sign of the green army. When it had been dark for over an hour, Gurion asked, "What were you supposed to do after it got dark?"

Dorothy shook her head, "She didn't say. She just said to stay here."

Another hour passed. Then the young woman returned.

"Emuna will see you now. Follow close behind me. And if for any reason we should get separated, stay away from the fences."

The young woman moved quickly out into the night. She led them through a labyrinth of tents, a maze that seldom made contact with the main paths within the complex. Finally, they were ushered inside a small and shabby tent and introduced to a woman dressed in beggar's rags.

"My name is Emuna. Please make yourselves comfortable. My people and I apologize for the treatment you have received at the hands of our brothers and sisters, the green army."

"I'm afraid it was my yellow robe," Dorothy said. "We are the ones who owe you an apology. We are not really members of the remnant at all. Gurion misled the guards so that we would be brought here."

"My people are not as easily fooled as the green army." Emuna did not look like a person who could be deceived.

"But if you knew that we were not remnant, why did you take us in?" Gurion asked.

"We never turn away a stranger to the power ordained," Emuna answered mysteriously. "The remnant are a very diverse group. Some of our people were formerly guards of the green army sent here to spy on us. We even have members who were of the yellow-cloaked army. But in your case, the decision was easy. Even though you are not of our people, you are remnant already."

"No, you don't understand," Gurion insisted. "We are from a different dimension, a different world. We were sent here to learn about the power ordained."

"The remnant are not of one world or of one dimension. They are the faithful of every age." Emuna's soft voice held them captive. "You have proven yourselves faithful. Whether you realize it or not, you are, indeed, remnant."

Before Dorothy or Gurion could respond, Emuna continued.

"I'm afraid this is an honor that comes at great cost to you both. Because you are remnant, you are not safe here. We are as much the enemy of the green army as are those who wear the cloaks of yellow."

"They only make you their enemies because you refuse to support the war against evil," Gurion said.

"Yes, that's part of it," Emuna replied. "But I think the real reason they make us their enemies is because they fear us."

Dorothy was confused. "But why would they fear you? You are their prisoners."

"They fear us because they cannot control us," Emuna

said. "They can kill us, but they cannot control us. And if they kill too many of us they are afraid their own troops will revolt."

From their puzzled looks, Emuna could tell that Dorothy and Gurion didn't understand.

"The good army is living a lie. They claim to be fighting against evil. But every time their leaders execute one of us, their own people cry out against what they have done. As hard as they try to portray us as traitors, their people know the truth."

"But you *are* traitors!" Gurion was as shocked as Dorothy at having said this. But he couldn't help himself. Something didn't make sense to him. He had to know the truth. "You have refused to support the war against evil. Doesn't that make you traitors?"

"I suppose it does make us traitors to the cause of this unfortunate war, to the power that threatens and intimidates. No, we are not mindless patriots with unquestioning loyalty to the green banner." Emuna's expression was pained. "But we are faithful to what we believe."

Gurion was not satisfied. "But I know you hate evil. That's what I don't understand. You hate evil and yet you don't support the good army's efforts to destroy it."

Emuna smiled sympathetically. "You have experienced the vile grip of evil. You have felt its sting. And now you want to strike back. Your feelings of disgust and your determination to fight back are noble. We share those feelings. But evil cannot be overcome by power that threatens and intimidates."

After a pause, she continued.

"Evil is a cunning adversary. It would lure us into false obedience. It tempts us to make use of its own foul power in the name of good. But its power is addictive. It becomes an obsession. If we serve that power we are serving the very evil we seek to overcome."

"But there has to be a way to fight evil!" Gurion insisted. "You can't just stand by and let it take over the world!"

Emuna spoke quietly, patiently. "Evil feeds on power. As long as we trust in earthly power to overcome it, we are feeding it, not fighting it. Only the power ordained can overcome evil—"

"I'm not sure I understand exactly what you mean by the power ordained," Dorothy interrupted.

"My friend, surely you are no stranger to the power ordained," Emuna replied incredulously. "Neither of you would have found your way here were it not for its guiding principles. What do you think I mean?"

The words of the keeper of the mist came back to Dorothy. It was almost as if she could see them printed on the air. She spoke them out loud:

"Do not be fooled by the illusion that problems can be solved by brute force or that good can come of evil. The power ordained, the power you seek, has nothing to do with intimidation. It is not the power that frightens or threatens. It has nothing to do with weapons. It recognizes neither wealth nor position. When you find the power that empowers the weak, that stands helpless and yet firm against tyranny, that will not intimidate or be intimidated— this is the power you must retrieve."

Silence flooded the room.

After a space of time, Gurion spoke. "But how can power that stands helpless overcome the dreadful power of evil? How can it possibly win a victory, for the forces of good?"

"Perhaps you are looking in the wrong place for your victory," Emuna suggested. "The good army is prepared to sacrifice the lives of tens of thousands of its faithful to win this war against evil. And its troops are willing to die for what they believe. There is certainly something noble about that."

She gazed thoughtfully into the distance.

"But it is all very sad, really. All those people willing to die for their faith. But to live it? How many are prepared to live it?"

Gurion's head began to spin. Images of green and yellow filled his mind. He saw the specter of a terrible war. Everywhere he looked, he saw death and destruction.

In his vision the green army seemed to be winning. Even though casualties were extremely high among the green-robed troops, their forces were breaking through the lines of the yellow-cloaked army and slaying the yellow robes with their terrible weapons. A green victory seemed imminent.

But then a great yellow face rose in the sky—the face of evil. And it was smiling.

At that moment Gurion realized exactly what the remnant meant when they said there was no earthly power that could overcome evil. Evil was a shadow that no sword could pierce, no weapon could destroy.

As the insatiable power of the good army was increased against its evil enemy, as its fires were stoked to a fearful brightness, the shadow of evil grew ever greater. The will to power fed the very flames that cast evil's shadow on the world. There could be no victory through power.

Evil and the will to power were linked inseparably. They were one and the same. Gurion wondered at this shadowy curse of emptiness he saw projected on the world. The shadow of power, of evil, was certainly not without substance. It was a real threat, a bane that poisoned people's minds and polluted their souls. But it ruled through emptiness, through the lack of something that Gurion could not quite identify or name.

What was it that was lacking in this wretched world where power prevailed?

Then, in a flash of insight, Gurion knew what it was that he and Dorothy had been sent to retrieve. He understood the treasure, the power ordained. It was love. In this nightmare of earthly power, love was lacking; only the remnant kept its memory alive.

Love. Could it be brought back into this world? Could it fill the emptiness and reclaim its rightful throne? How would love be received by those who were faithful to the green banner, those who had been converted to the power of moral determination?

In a world where love ruled, there could be no will to power. Love would mean letting go. When the fires of power were allowed to die down, the shadow of evil would be diminished. Power was not the path to victory over evil. It sounded like foolishness, but victory would come only through emancipation from that power.

Gurion felt himself relaxing, letting go. The fears that

had stalked him so relentlessly rose up once again in a parade of images: bent shapes, shadows of the island, spidery figures, giant lizards with great wings. Gurion let them pass.

Then evil confronted him with its empty hood and its yellow eyes. For a second, Gurion felt his old rage begin to rise up. He wanted to strike out at the hooded figure. But he did not. Instead he took a deep breath and let go of his rage.

The hooded figure reached out and took hold of Gurion's shoulders, near his neck. Gurion could feel the spidery fingers piercing his green robe. He had felt the sting of evil before, the poison of fear. Only this time he was not afraid.

"Gurion! Are you all right?" It was Dorothy's voice, Dorothy's hands on his shoulders shaking him gently. "We are back on the island."

It was morning, a new day. The first rays of the sun danced like hope through the entrance of the cave.

8

$\mathcal{S}$HARING

The island was a world unto itself, a magical world where all things were possible. Gurion and Dorothy had been called into its enchantment, chosen to be servants of the mist and seekers of the true service.

Somehow, their quests had become entangled. Through the timelessness of the Hall of Service, the voice had called them together to share adventures that would prepare them for service in their own worlds.

Now the time had come to test what they had learned. Through the morning fog they trudged with Kendra, the gatekeeper, to the testing ground that had been ordained by the voice.

In the heart of the island was a clearing. A large arena had been built in the very center of this clearing, marked off with a circle of stones and filled with a mixture of sand and sawdust. A hand-hewn log bench faced the empty arena.

Dorothy and Gurion knew only that some kind of tournament would take place in the arena to test their understanding of the true service. If Kendra knew any details of the contest, she had not divulged them.

Gurion had visited the arena once before and had sat on the bench. Later, he had described his experience to Kendra. She told him then that the log bench was enchanted, that the images he experienced there were illusions. He had only recently come to terms with those fearful images.

For Dorothy the trip to the center of the island, and to the enchanted arena, was a first. She had not shared Gurion's frightening experience there, nor did she share his belief in the mythical creatures alleged to inhabit the island.

Kendra led them toward the arena in a strict discipline of silence. She insisted that a two-hour silent march would help prepare them for the ordeal they would face.

Both Dorothy and Gurion were dressed in their robes of hope.

As they walked, Dorothy's thoughts kept coming back to the words the keeper of the mist had used to address the voice: *Ministrare est vivere.* She recalled how the words had woven themselves around her, how they had danced in the air.

When she had first seen these words carved in the ornate arch outside the Hall of Service she had not understood their meaning. Only at the hot spring had the meaning of the words been revealed to her. *Ministrare est vivere:* To serve is to live.

She knew that the words were more than just an ancient motto chiseled in the cold stone of the Hall of Service. They were the guiding force of all who pledged their lives to the voice's call. "To serve is to live." Words of promise. Words of hope.

During the two-hour silence, Gurion's mind was filled with questions. He did not feel ready to be tested. As he remembered the challenges he had faced, it seemed obvious to him that he would never have made it this far if it were not for Dorothy. She had all the right instincts to serve the voice. He was always stumbling. Why had the voice called him, of all people?

He had come to the island in ignorance. He knew nothing of what it meant to serve the voice when he arrived. Now, already, his understanding of true service would be put to the test. Even after all the adventures he and Dorothy had shared, he was not sure what was required of him. Sometimes the idea of serving the voice seemed like an impossible task.

The mist was just beginning to lift by the time the three of them reached the clearing. It was late morning. Kendra led them to the arena but did not seat them on the hand-hewn log. She turned to them and broke the silence.

"You have been initiated into the ways of service. We are here today to discover what you have learned and to determine if it is time for me to lead you back into the world."

"How will we be tested?" Dorothy asked.

"The tests you face will be of your own choosing. Every

image that challenges you will come from within your being. Each of us has only one true teacher, and it is that teacher who will do the testing. Just as you had to find your own way through the various adventures you faced, you must now decide for yourself what those adventures have taught you about the true service."

"What if we fail the test?" Gurion had to swallow hard before asking the question.

"The only way you can fail the test is by refusing to take it." Kendra's eyes were smiling. "The voice calls no one to failure."

The arena was still adrift with mist, but in the sky Gurion saw patches of blue. It reminded him of the day he had first come to the island. How long ago had that been?

Kendra moved toward the arena. Dorothy followed. As much as Gurion would have liked to stand pat, he knew the time had come to face his doubts.

As Gurion hesitantly took his position on the rough-shaped bench, a flood of memories returned. But to his great relief, most of them were positive. He sensed again the strong feeling of home that he had known that first day. He was no stranger here. He belonged on this bench. He felt loved and accepted. He felt valued.

The memories of the images that had frightened him were pale by contrast. They had lost their grip, or perhaps it was he who had learned to let them go. A calmness surrounded him. He took a deep breath and let it out slowly, ready to face whatever it was that awaited him.

Out of the creeping mist of the arena an imposing figure

walked. He wore a coarsely woven cloak of homespun yarn that bore an intricate pattern blended of several shades of blue and gold. And he walked with an air of authority.

"Come, my friends, the games are ready for you."

Gurion and Dorothy got up from the bench and walked warily into the arena.

"Before we begin, it is important that you understand the object of the game and the rules of play," the figure in blue and gold explained. "You will each be challenged by a worthy adversary and judged according to your valor. If you overcome your opponent, by whatever means, it will be a sign to us that you are ready to return to your world in the noble service of the voice.

"If you fail to overcome your opponent, you will be given the option of continuing your quest for true service or of being returned to your world through the one-way door in the Hall of Service. If you return to your world through the one-way door, all memory of these adventures will be forgotten. Is that clear?"

Both Dorothy and Gurion nodded.

"There is only one rule that must be followed. But the consequences of disobeying it are dire indeed," he continued. "Each of you must meet your adversary alone. To come to the assistance of your companion is a crime punishable by banishment from the order of service. Should you commit such a crime you will be defrocked and sent home in shame. You will retain full memory of these adventures. And you will never be able to forget the grave sin that led to your expulsion from the order."

There was a pause while the man in the mantle of blue and gold mumbled some words to counteract even the mention of such a blasphemous possibility. Then he continued.

"If such an unlikely event should transpire, your companion will not be penalized. Such actions will be considered proof of worthiness, and your companion will be awarded the high honor of induction into the order of service—in spite of any failure to overcome the designated adversary."

After the rules of play had been explained, Gurion and Dorothy were taken to opposite ends of the arena and given shining swords and shields inscribed with the motto *Ministrare est vivere.* Then the captain of the tournament disappeared into the fog in the center of the arena.

While Gurion awaited his challenge, he tried his sword. It was a superb instrument, forged of a lightweight alloy and perfectly balanced. He wondered what kind of adversary he would face.

But before he could even imagine any possibilities, he heard words of dark accusation. "We meet again, intruder!"

Gurion recognized the vile tone of the one who spoke. Even before he turned to confront his accuser, an image was already beginning to form in his mind. Even so, he was not prepared for the evil gaze of the yellow eyes that stared hatefully at him from the empty shadow of a hooded tunic.

Gurion looked at his sword. He knew it was useless against the shadow of evil. It was a shining symbol of power, but power only intensified evil's shadow.

Curiously, he was not afraid. His adventures had prepared him well for this adversary. He knew exactly what he must do. Assuming a defensive posture, he refused to strike out in anger. He used his shield and sword to protect himself from the spidery figure's lunges, but he would not allow himself to be lured into a self-righteous rage. Within minutes the figure with the yellow eyes began to fade. Gurion's shield and sword absorbed its frantic blows until it disappeared completely.

Then all was quiet. Gurion stood with his sword trailing harmlessly at his side.

This was it?

He couldn't believe he had met his challenge so easily. He had overcome his opponent. He would be returned to his world in service of the voice. He would be commissioned into the order of service.

Gurion's thoughts turned to Dorothy. He wondered how she was faring. Out of curiosity, he decided to walk to the opposite side of the arena to watch. The mist was still heavy in the center of the arena, but cleared as he approached the end where Dorothy's challenge faced her.

And what a challenge it was! Her adversary was a huge dragon that stood as tall as a house. Its green scales were as thick as plate armor. Compared to the dragon, Dorothy looked like a mouse facing a large cat.

The dragon was toying with her, batting her around with its huge head as if it were trying to get her to spar, to go through futile motions of attack and defense. But Dorothy was in a stupor. She was groggy and muddle-headed.

Gurion could see it was only a matter of time until the dragon tired of the game and finished her off with one swipe of its clawed foot.

What was wrong? Why did she refuse even to raise her shield for protection?

Then Gurion realized the problem. Dorothy didn't believe in dragons or other mythological creatures. She was completely unprepared for such a challenge because it was outside the range of what her mind would allow possible. Reduced to paralysis because of her fear, she was about to be overcome.

The sight of Dorothy so completely helpless against her foe was more than Gurion could bear. How many times had she come to his aid when he needed her? How many times had she kept him from doing the wrong thing? And now she desperately needed his help.

Gurion thought about the rules of the arena. He knew he had been forbidden to aid her in any way. He had defeated his opponent and was assured of induction into the order of service if he did nothing to help her. He would be relinquishing all that if he came to her assistance. He would be sent home in shame.

The dragon nudged her again with its nose. Its red eyes flared. Then it raised its wings and cast a huge shadow over Dorothy's frail form. The game was about to be concluded.

Gurion sprang to Dorothy's side just as the dragon pounced. He raised his shield and sword in a vain attempt to guard her from the beast's descent. The underside of the dragon was not protected with scales. Gurion's sword penetrated the soft flesh and pierced the dragon's heart.

In an explosion of pain the dragon leaped away from the two companions dressed so vulnerably in their robes of hope. But it was too late for escape. The wound was fatal. Within moments the beast lay dead on the ground.

Both Dorothy and Gurion had been nearly crushed by the weight of the dragon. The heavy burden had temporarily knocked them out. When Gurion came to, Dorothy had been taken away. And Kendra had presumably gone with her. Standing over him was the captain of the tournament.

"Is she okay?" Gurion asked.

"A little bruised, but she will be fine." The captain was not smiling.

"She doesn't believe in dragons. She didn't know what to do. I was afraid the dragon would kill her." Gurion thought of Dorothy standing so helplessly before her winged adversary. "She would have done the same for me."

"That doesn't alter your situation. You broke the rules and you must suffer the consequences." The captain's voice was stern. "Were my instructions clear? Did you understand the part about not coming to the assistance of your companion?"

"Yes, I think so," Gurion said.

"And did you understand the consequences of such a deed?"

Gurion got to his feet. "Yes, I am to be banished from the island, banished from the order of service."

"When laws are broken, justice demands retribution. You broke the rules of the tournament. Now face the punishment ordained." The captain's expression was fierce. "Your canoe is where you left it. I trust you can find your way back to it. And you may never return to this island as long as you live. Do you understand?"

"Yes. I'm sorry. I really wanted to serve the voice more than anything in the world. But . . . I just couldn't turn my back on her. I'm sorry."

The captain's expression did not change. Gurion sought in vain for any sign of mercy or understanding. There was none. He saw only the captain's firm resolve to see justice done. "Your robe. I must insist that you remove it."

Gurion took off the robe and folded it carefully for the last time. Then he turned away and started the long walk back to the peninsula where he had left his canoe, an eternity ago.

As he walked, his adventures with Dorothy flooded his mind. He thought of Wilfred, the knight, of Olena and the community of hope. He thought of Cara's world and the old weeping oak. He remembered the presence of the voice coming to them in the whirlwind, calling them to service. He beheld the keeper of the mist, the armies of good and evil. He could see Emuna of the remnant as clearly as if she stood before him. And Kendra. Through it all he could see the gentle face of Kendra, and hear her healing songs.

Lost in his memories, the long trail back to the canoe seemed shorter. Before he knew it, the path narrowed into the jutting finger of the peninsula. The waters of the lake were choppy. An afternoon wind was rising.

He found his canoe just as he had left it. His work here

was finished. All that remained was to paddle back to the world he had left behind and take up his life where he had left it. The island was a chronicle of tales that had all been told. It was behind him now, the stuff of fable and legend, the realm of what might have been.

He pushed away from the island into the unsettled waters. Only once did he look back over his shoulder to survey his loss. His eyes were blurred with tears, but they were not tears of regret. He knew he would never regret coming to Dorothy's aid. No, these were tears of farewell. The island had become an old friend, and it was hard saying good-bye to a friend.

As he paddled back to the mainland through the waters of fear, the afternoon winds increased. The windswept waters of the lake pitched and battered his canoe. A storm was coming.

Gurion struggled to keep afloat. He thought about turning back to the island, but he knew that was impossible. So he did his best to hold his course. Eventually the winds blew with such force that he forgot about everything but the waters of fear. His canoe was half full of water now. He put down his paddle and tried desperately to bale water out of the canoe with his hands. It was a losing cause. He was sinking.

The last thing he remembered was his paddle floating beside him as the canoe capsized. Then he was alone in the water. He slapped frantically and gasped for breath, but his panic pulled him down into the stormy waters of fear.

When he opened his eyes, Gurion thought he must

surely have drowned and gone wherever it is people go when they have died. He was lying on a soft mattress covered with sheets that smelled sweet and clean. A child kept watch over him. By the look on her face he could tell she was surprised to see him stirring.

"Hello," he said. "Who are you?"

Without answering the child jumped up and ran from the room. Within minutes she returned with an old man with a white beard. The little girl stood behind the old man and peeked out from behind him at Gurion.

"So, you are not ready for the grave after all!" the old man teased.

"What happened?" Gurion said weakly.

"I'm afraid that is a story you will have to tell us. Sara found your body on the beach after the storm. We thought you were dead. You swallowed a lot of water, but you were still breathing. So we brought you here. It has been almost three days."

"Where am I?" Gurion asked.

"You are in the land of Ministrare, the land under the waters. You will be well cared for here. The important thing now is to help you get your strength back." The old man whispered something in the little girl's ear, and she ran out of the room again. "Do you feel like eating something?"

Suddenly Gurion realized how hungry he was. "Yes, thank you—"

"Leben. My name is Leben."

"I feel so weak." Gurion tried to sit up, but his head started spinning.

"Sara will bring you some broth. It would be best if you allowed her to feed it to you at first. I will be back after you have eaten. We can talk more then."

Over the next several days the old man came often. Little by little, Gurion felt his strength returning. He told his story to Leben: his call to the island, his adventures with Dorothy, his banishment. Through it all the old man listened intently.

"It is a strange world you come from, my young friend."

"Yes, the Hall of Service does sound a bit strange, I guess," Gurion admitted.

"No, I'm talking about the world that understands justice as punishment," Leben explained.

Gurion had never really thought much about it. But it didn't seem strange to him to think of justice as a system of laws and consequences. He wondered what the old man meant but did not ask.

When Gurion had recovered sufficiently, Leben and Sara took him for long walks in the land of Ministrare. Sara played games with him and raced with him through the woods. Gurion had never seen a people so content, so generous. Everywhere he went he was met with outgoing love and generosity. Leben himself had given Gurion everything he needed, more than he needed. And not out of a sense of duty but willingly, even eagerly—as if Gurion were his own son.

One time he asked Leben what made the people so generous.

"Generous?" Leben asked, as if he did not know the

meaning of the word. "Is it generous to share what God has freely given us? Can I be called generous for sharing what belongs to God?"

By the bemused look on Gurion's face, Leben could tell that Gurion did not grasp what he was saying.

"What God has given us, we are charged to use faithfully," Leben explained. "And to share freely. There is only One who is truly generous. The world belongs to God. We are but caretakers of God's world, charged to extend the love and generosity we have experienced to others."

Gurion could see that Leben was serious. "Where I come from, most people get pretty possessive about what God has given them. It is considered generous even to share a small portion of those possessions."

Leben was puzzled. "Don't your people feel an obligation to share what God has given them?"

Gurion thought for a moment. "I suppose some of them feel that way. But mostly they cling to what they know is rightfully theirs. I guess they are afraid someone will take it away from them."

"Yours is a strange world indeed," Leben muttered, shaking his head. "A world with no sense of justice."

Now Gurion was puzzled. "What do you mean?"

"Justice. Oh, I forgot. Your people don't think of justice in the same way we do." Leben sought for a new word.

"But surely justice is justice," Gurion said. "Justice is fair treatment under the law."

"We don't understand justice in a legal sense at all," Leben said. "To us, justice is a matter of relationship."

"Relationship?" Gurion asked.

"Yes. And sharing. Justice is sharing God's gifts, sharing the world God has given us, extending God's love and generosity responsibly and fairly."

"But what about laws?" Gurion asked. "Don't you have laws to protect people?"

"We have laws," Leben explained. "But a person can follow all the laws and still not behave justly. And the courts can administer the laws with justice or without justice. Laws demand punishment for broken rules. Justice demands that broken relationships be mended. We believe in punishment. But we don't confuse it with justice."

"I'm afraid I am still a bit confused," Gurion admitted.

Leben searched for a way to make Gurion understand. "We call our land Ministrare. Do you know what that means?"

Gurion shook his head.

"*Ministrare* means 'to serve,'" Leben clarified. "This is the land of true service."

Gurion's world began to spin. True service . . . true service . . . The words spun around him in a vortex of color, a whirlwind of inspiration and hope.

"True service . . . true service . . ." He heard the words, but at first he did not recognize the voice that spoke them. Then he realized it was his own. He opened his eyes to see if the spinning had stopped. Before him he saw the arena. The mist had lifted. The arena was empty of anything but sand and sawdust. Kendra sat beside him, her eyes just beginning to open. And beyond Kendra sat Dorothy.

Illusion. It was all an illusion. There had been no spidery figure. No dragon. There had been no banishment. And there had been no land of Ministrare.

But what of the part about true service? Kendra had said that Gurion's test would come from within himself. Had he imagined it all? What did it mean?

Dorothy was back now; her eyes had opened. Kendra got up from the bench and walked silently away, deep in her own thoughts. Gurion wanted to speak, to ask Dorothy about her experience in the arena, but somehow he knew that the enchantment she had faced belonged to her alone.

The arena, the testing ground, was quiet. Not an image stirred on its blank surface. Gurion knew he had discovered something important there. A key to understanding himself, his call to service. The quest for the true service had brought him ultimately here, to the realm of his imagination.

"The time has come for the greatest adventure of all." It was Kendra who spoke. "I am to lead you to the hollow tree where all will be revealed. The voice calls you back to your own worlds."

Gurion felt ready to leave. He knew he had only glimpsed the important dimensions of what his call to service involved. Yet that flash of insight had forever changed the way he would view his world. His quest for the true service had transformed him in ways he could not yet imagine.

However, in spite of all that had happened, there was much that Gurion did not understand. He was like a toddler learning to walk. The steps he had taken were crucial to his development. But in the greater scheme of things they were mere baby steps.

The impressions he had formed of the true service were nebulous. They lacked a definite form. Somehow he had to make sense of these fragments and fashion them into a model of service that would be a guiding force in his life. Gurion wondered what Kendra meant by the hollow tree where all would be revealed. But he did not ask. Kendra rarely wasted words on things she could not explain.

The way to the hollow tree lay to the west. The three walked silently as before. Gurion thought about the land of Ministrare, the land of true service. It seemed so real to him. Was it possible that Leben had been right about justice? Leben spoke of justice and sharing in the same breath. He understood justice as an attitude that compelled a person to share God's gifts responsibly and fairly.

In all of Gurion's life he had never heard the idea of justice presented in this way. He had always thought of justice as the right to a fair trial, as a system of laws and consequences. Could it be that a just world involved more than the enforcement of laws?

How could these two worlds, these two entirely different ways of seeing, be brought together? How could Leben's sense of justice be established in Gurion's world? These were some of the things that were on Gurion's mind as he walked toward the hollow tree.

Dorothy, like Gurion, reflected on the experience that had tested her.

On her way to the arena she had been thinking about the meaning of the words *Ministrare est vivere.* It had been revealed to her that these words, so mysterious when she first saw them chiseled in stone, were the guiding force of all who pledged their lives to the voice's call. As a motto they meant something like "To serve is to live," but Dorothy knew that they were much more than just an ancient motto.

When Dorothy sat down on the enchanted bench, she was fairly certain that the test she was about to face would have something to do with the significance of these words.

A child had greeted Dorothy in the arena. In each hand the child held a gift. One gift was wrapped in silver and gold with a ribbon of precious jewels. It glimmered and sparkled in the sunlight, and Dorothy could not take her eyes off it.

The other gift was poorly wrapped. In fact, the wrapping was coming off in places, and Dorothy could see that its contents were a washbasin and towel.

Dorothy was about to choose the glittering gift of gold when she noticed that the child's face needed washing. On impulse she chose the washbasin, instead, and gently washed the child's face.

Then the child opened the silver and gold wrappings and revealed the contents of the first gift. It contained a scroll with the words MINISTRARE EST VIVERE boldly printed at the top. Dorothy could see that it was some kind of secret pledge, a pledge for membership into the order of service.

The child opened the scroll, read the pledge, and presented the scroll to Dorothy for her signature. After she had signed it, a light like a long stairway came down from the heavens. The child hugged Dorothy and then walked up the stairs, taking the scroll with her.

It was this pledge that Dorothy reflected on as she walked silently toward the hollow tree. The fact that the whole experience might have been an illusion or enchantment never even crossed her mind.

–Isaac Watts (1674–1748), "Psalm 90"

9

PROMISE

Gurion stood spellbound before the hollow tree, transfixed by what he had just witnessed. Moments after she had entered the empty cavity of the tree's broad trunk, Dorothy had shimmered, faded, and then disappeared forever into her own world.

"She takes with her all she has experienced here and everything the tree has been witness to through its centuries of service as a passageway."

Kendra's words were reassuring, but Gurion could not take his eyes off the hollow space where Dorothy had stood. The tree's stark emptiness reflected his own feelings. Dorothy was gone and would never return.

He missed her already. They had said their good-byes, shared their insights one last time about the meaning of the voice's call.

She had written out the pledge for him, as close as she could remember it. Even now he held it in his hand. It was titled "MINISTRARE EST VIVERE." To serve is to live. And its well-chosen words made clear and orderly the cloudy impressions he had formed of the true service.

"Where will she reenter her world?" Gurion asked, still half expecting her to reappear.

"She will enter her world at precisely the moment and place she first met you. She will awake, as if from a dream. But she will forget nothing."

Gurion remembered the grassy meadow in the enchanted forest where the blue fish had led him. He could still picture Dorothy's campfire and the large stack of dead branches she had gathered, her only security against an uncertain future. He recalled adding a branch to the smoldering fire just before they had met. He hoped it burned warmly for her now as she awoke.

Kendra continued. "The life she returns to will be exactly the same as it was the moment she left it. But she will be changed. She returns, as will you, entrusted with a sacred duty."

Gurion wondered what it all meant. Growing up in the church, he had been told repeatedly that he was created in the image of God. Until now, these words had meant little to him. They were words crusty with the outdated traditions of the past, words covered with so many barnacles that no one really seemed to understand them anymore.

More than anything he could think of, it was service that

characterized the God who had called him. If there were an image of God emblazoned in the hearts of humanity, it seemed to Gurion it would bear the stamp of service. Could it be that the mark of true service he and Dorothy were to carry in their lives was nothing other than this very image of God itself?

Certainly the image of true service was a torch they had been commissioned to carry into the world. It had become their responsibility, their sacred duty to bear this light in the midst of a world that had forgotten humanity's true purpose.

They were called to act as lighthouses in a fogbound world, as God's servants of the mist. Yet if humanity had once been gifted with the stamp of service, the world had rejected this image in favor of images "more befitting" their God—images of kingliness and immortality, images of power and retribution. But these images, in human beings at least, did not reflect God's will. They were false images for humanity. They carried no redeeming life.

Both Gurion and Dorothy had come a long way to the hollow tree. Their adventures had taught them much, but Gurion still wondered what would really be required of them back in their own worlds.

Dorothy had her formal pledge tucked safely away in her memory. She confessed to Gurion that she had repeated it several times to herself on the way to the hollow tree, just to be sure she would not forget any part of it.

Gurion read the words, again, to himself. Certainly, this was a pledge to live by. But the very fact that Dorothy had worked so hard to commit it to memory pointed out a shortcoming. It was external. As hard as she had tried to internalize it, it remained something outside of herself.

Gurion was convinced that the stamp of true service, the image of God, had to be an internal thing. It could not be a pledge—not even a pledge written on a scroll of gold. No, the true service was something that was written on a person's heart.

"Are you ready, my friend, to begin your journey?" Kendra's hand was on his shoulder.

There was still so much he didn't know. The reality of what he had been charged to do and the seeming impossibility of living up to that charge concerned him. But he knew that nothing Kendra could say now would lighten the burden he felt.

"Yes, I am ready." And with those words he stepped cautiously, reverently, into the hollow tree as if it were a house of worship, as if the rustle of its leaves were the Word of the God who had called him.

The sound of the wind caused Gurion to stiffen a little in anticipation, of what he didn't know. Perhaps he should expect a shower of color and light. Or maybe he would be plunged again into the now familiar realm of suffocating darkness that surrounded the Hall of Service. Seconds ticked into minutes. He felt nothing, experienced nothing.

The trunk of the tree encircled him with an aura of warmth and security. He waited, somewhat impatiently, in the safe haven of this pithy womb to be reborn. But nothing happened.

Why? He had seen Dorothy fade and disappear with his own eyes. And hadn't Kendra said that everything the tree had been witness to would be revealed?

Still nothing.

He wondered if he should leave the hollow of the tree and seek Kendra's guidance, but he wasn't sure what would happen if he did. He looked out through the fire-darkened opening of the hollow trunk to see if he could locate Kendra, but Kendra was not there.

Gurion stepped cautiously from the tree so he could find Kendra and discover what had gone wrong. But even before he had a chance to get his bearings, the hollow tree shimmered, faded, and then disappeared exactly as Dorothy had.

Gurion felt a chill. He knew something was wrong. He seemed to be back in his own world; he recognized some of the natural landmarks around him. The mountains in the distance looked right. The lakeshore seemed familiar. But the trees were wrong. It was as if he had been away for a generation or more.

The part of the shoreline where Gurion had begun his odyssey, where he stood now, had been logged a few years before Gurion's birth. The trees, as Gurion remembered them, were small- to medium-sized pines and firs. But these trees were much larger and much more numerous.

How long had he been away? Had he, too, changed as the forest before him? He hurried down to the waters of the lake and knelt to see his reflection. A stranger's middle-aged face stared back at him. Gurion brought his hand slowly to his cheek to explore the bearded face he saw. He stroked the whiskers warily and then splashed his face with the cold water of the lake. But when the waters had settled, the image of the stranger remained.

He knew he had to find a way back to the hollow tree. If only Dorothy were here. Her instincts, usually better than his, would surely point them in the right direction. But this time he was on his own. He felt alone, abandoned.

And yet Gurion was not entirely alone. Even though, in his impatience, he had broken faith and left the hollow tree before its promise could be fulfilled, the one who had called him had not broken faith with Gurion. As Kendra had promised, Gurion could not be separated from the experiences of the island, from the lessons the voice had taught.

As he walked the main path through the woods, Gurion assessed his situation. From the look of his reflection he appeared to be in his mid-thirties. The only good he could see in that was that the years made a terrific disguise. He had arrived complete with a trimmed beard and mustache. No one would recognize him.

He didn't have any money, so he would need to find someone he could trust, somewhere to stay. Home was a possibility, of course. But how many years had it been since his mother had lost all hope of seeing him again? And Gurion was determined to find the hollow tree. He couldn't bear the thought of breaking her heart again. And yet, he needed to see her and know she was all right.

His mind kept returning to his best friend in the world,

Karyn Evans. But surely she would be grown and would have moved away by now. Perhaps his mother would know where she had gone. It seemed a long shot, but if Karyn were still in town he knew he could trust her to help.

Along the way, Gurion noticed that his world had aged with him; still, it remained more recognizable than he. The threshold of the third millennium had been crossed nearly two decades ago. However, there seemed to be little evidence of it. The road back to town had been widened and a bike path added. The cars were sleeker and quieter, but they still looked much the same.

In the last decade of the twentieth century there had been a plague of despair foretelling an end to the world—an end that was supposed to coincide with the beginning of the third millennium. All the prophets of the day had predicted it. Gurion had never bought into their despair. He had imagined instead the birth of great scientific advancements, the stuff of science fiction, to solve the indisputable problems of the day.

But as far as Gurion could tell, the beginning of the third millennium had brought humanity neither catastrophe nor salvation. What it had brought instead was hope. There seemed to be no rational explanation for the hope he felt, and he did not entirely understand it. Nevertheless, just as every sunrise holds the promise of a new day and every New Year's Eve the promise of a new year, the dawn of a new millennium holds its own promise—the hope of another thousand years.

Gurion could not escape the feeling that humanity had

been offered a great gift. Without a doubt, human beings had stumbled through the last thousand years avoiding their true destiny. But did not the gift of this new millennium offer sure evidence of the prodigal faithfulness of the Creator? Never mind the broken promises of humanity's past. The future offered hope.

When Gurion arrived at his street, he walked more slowly, amazed at the subtle changes on his block. The yards he knew so well, that he had played in for all the years he could remember, did not welcome him anymore. Time had made him a stranger here. He could not even recognize his own house. At first he thought it might have been torn down and a new one built in its place. The number was right. The door was in the same place. But nothing looked familiar.

He made himself ring the bell before he had time to consider the consequences. Only after he had rung it did he begin to panic.

"Yes?" His mother looked cautiously past the edge of the door, the pain of the years evident in her face.

"I—uh, I'm looking for Karyn Evans. I must have the wrong house," Gurion stammered.

"Who is it, Penny?" a voice asked from another room. It was the voice of his stepfather. Gurion's panic increased. "Open the door."

"I don't want to let Argus out, John. I'm afraid he'll wander off again."

Argus, just a puppy when Gurion had left for the island, stuck his gray muzzle through the doorway and sniffed Gurion. He whimpered and wagged his tail before being dragged back into the house. It was all Gurion could do to keep from dropping to his knees and hugging his dog.

"Hmm. Karyn Evans. Her family used to live next door. We still get a Christmas card from her. Let me see if I can find her new address for you." His mother disappeared into the house for a few minutes and then returned to the door. "She lives just a couple of blocks west of here on Blackberry Circle. Here, I wrote it down for you."

"Thanks for your help," Gurion said, turning his head so she would not notice the tears that were beginning to form in his eyes. Just as the door was about to be closed, Argus ran through the opening and lay down at Gurion's feet. Gurion knelt and stroked the old dog's head.

"I'm sorry. He's usually not this friendly with strangers," Gurion's mother said. "It's almost as if he knows you."

"He's a great dog," Gurion said, as much to Argus as to his mother. "He reminds me of a dog I had when I was a kid."

Gurion walked the three blocks to Blackberry Drive and then about half a block more to Blackberry Circle. He found the address written on the paper his mother had given him and rang the doorbell.

A woman in her mid-thirties, whom Gurion recognized immediately as Karyn, answered the door. She looked hard at him. "I'm sorry, do I know you?"

"You used to. We were old friends about twenty years ago." Gurion tried to smile. "I don't know how to tell you this without its being a shock, but—"

"Gurion? Gurion!" She stepped out onto the porch,

holding him at arm's length. Then she walked around him, looking at him from all sides. "Everyone thought you were dead. But I knew. . . . I just knew it wasn't true. Does your mother know you're back? Have you seen her?"

"No. Uh—well, yes. I mean, I stopped by the house to get your address and to be sure she was all right, but she didn't recognize me and I didn't know how to tell her what happened."

"Come in. You can practice on me. I want to know everything."

Gurion spent the next few hours trying to make sense of all that had happened to him. He watched Karyn's face as he spoke. No one could possibly believe what I'm saying, he thought. She's going to think I'm crazy. But her eyes never showed any measure of doubt. She laughed with him and cried with him. When he got to the part about stepping out of the hollow tree before it was time, she gasped "No!" and her eyes filled with tears.

Gurion stayed with Karyn for more than a week. She told him all that had happened in her life. Her parents had been killed when she was still in high school. Her aunt had taken her in and helped her get through college. She loved horses and kept three of them stabled at the edge of town. She took Gurion to see them and made him promise to go riding with her before he left.

Gurion began to worry about ever finding the way back to the hollow tree. He wondered if he was here to stay.

Then came the storm.

It seemed, at first, to be just another summer

thunderstorm. And yet no heavy rains came. It was spectacular at night. Lightning danced incessantly, high in the distant sky, and the growl of thunder never stopped.

According to the news, some unusual activity on the sun—solar flares larger than a dozen earths—was causing a magnetic storm. At first the reports promised that the storm's effects were temporary and no cause for alarm. But every night the auroras grew brighter and more animated. The lights shimmered and jumped, faded and disappeared, only to come back more brightly than before.

During the daylight hours the auroras were not visible. But soon the daytime lightning also increased. Strange cloud formations began to appear, and the mist distorted the eerie light show, blurring its colors and muffling its roar.

Within a couple of days, television and radio signals became so jumbled that reception faded and then sizzled into a meaningless hiss. Soon after, surges in power lines blew transformers until much of the earth was without electricity. Emergency gasoline generators still functioned, but no one knew for how long.

Through it all, Gurion tried to make sense of what was happening. He looked for a sign of promise. Surely the God who had gifted humanity with the birth of a new millennium could be counted on no matter how bad things got; of that, Gurion had no doubt. But where was the sign, and what was Gurion's place in all of this?

Finally, in the midst of the storm, Gurion raised his arms to the sky and called on the voice.

Karyn watched in awe as a rainbow of light formed an

arc around him. From where she stood it appeared as if Gurion were lifted off the ground with the force of the light. At first she thought he had been struck by lightning. But he remained standing in the middle of the bow of color, his arms aimed at the sky, as if he were an arrow about to be unloosed.

Gurion did not see the rainbow that embraced him, but he heard the voice. "I can send you back now, Gurion. You are not ready for what will be asked of you. When you have lived the twenty years that were taken from you, perhaps then you will be ready. It is your choice. But I must warn you. The way will not be easy, and, should you fail, all will be lost."

"But how could I live my life knowing the earth would be threatened by this storm and worrying if I would be ready for it?" Gurion asked. "What kind of life would that be? No, if I am being given the choice, I will stay and face the storm now."

"Then there is no time to lose. There will be a short break in the storm in a few hours. When that occurs you need to be positioned at the old lighthouse at North Point. Do you know the place?"

"Yes," Gurion answered, remembering the old lighthouse and how far away it was. Even twenty years ago the roads had been closed to traffic. About the only way to reach North Point was by boat. But to be on the waters in this storm? Surely there must be some other way.

"In the tower of the lighthouse you will find a ring. Go to the roof of the lighthouse and hold the ring as high as you can until it catches the rays of the sun. Do you understand, Gurion?"

"Yes, I think so."

"You must be positioned exactly as I have told you at precisely the time the storm breaks. At that moment the moon will be directly overhead, though you may be unable to see it."

Karyn had moved closer to Gurion, as close as she dared. He seemed to be suspended in the rainbow of light. She could see that he was talking to someone, but she could not hear what was being said. She moved closer still, until she could just make out the words.

"Beware, Gurion. The task you undertake is a grave responsibility. The sudden burst of energy through the ring could consume you if you are not ready."

The arc of colors that held Gurion shimmered and then moved away from him and into the sky. Gurion's body relaxed and then slumped to the ground. Karyn rushed to him seeing that he was all right, sat beside him. She could find no words to express her awe, so she sat in silence.

Finally Gurion spoke. "I must get to the old lighthouse as soon as possible. The only way I know to get there is by boat, and I don't even know where to get a boat."

Karyn could see the weariness in Gurion's face, even though his journey had not yet begun. "I know a better way," she said, with some hesitation, watching Gurion's expression. "We can get there by the old road."

"Has the road been repaired since we were kids?" Gurion asked, surprised.

"No, it is still impassable by car," Karyn said. "But we would not be in a car. We would be on horses."

The weariness faded from Gurion's face and was replaced by a smile. "Your horses—of course!"

"From the stable we can cut directly across the hills to the north, until we come to the old road, and then follow it to North Point. I have ridden across those hills many times." Karyn could see that Gurion's expression had changed. "What's wrong?"

"The storm. It's going to be a very dangerous trip for us and the horses. I have no right to ask you—"

"You *didn't* ask me." Karyn smiled as she cut him off. "I offered. Now let's get moving."

The road to the stable was completely deserted. The storm had mesmerized the whole town, no doubt the entire world. The strange formations of lightning had moved lower in the sky and were striking the earth much more frequently. The rain increased.

Karyn saddled Athena, her black Morgan mare, for Gurion. Athena did not seem to be as bothered by the storm as the other two horses. For herself she saddled Lunar Tides, whom she called Shooter. Shooter's eyes were wide with fear. He tilted his head and looked sideways at Karyn as she outfitted him for the long ride. Karyn patted his chubby white-blazed face and spoke softly to him. He seemed to respond to her calming influence. His sleek brown body relaxed, but his eyes were as wild as the storm.

Once past the familiar grounds around the stable, the two riders headed due north, toward the steep hills that stood between them and North Point. Karyn led the way, following a trail that had meandered through these hills for a thousand years.

The rains were heavier now. Karyn had a poncho in one of her saddlebags, but Gurion was drenched to the bone. The clouds had settled heavily on the hills, and as they made their ascent they rode through patches of gray fog.

Lightning flashed incessantly in the distance. The riders could feel their horses tense with every flash. With every peal of thunder the horses spooked and tried to turn back to the safety of the stable. But somehow Karyn kept Shooter headed toward North Point, toward the old lighthouse, and Athena followed.

When they finally reached the top of the trail and began their descent, Karyn dismounted to give the horses a breather. Looking down the trail to the north, Gurion could see that the fog was worsening. The lightning strikes were closer now, and it looked as if they would be traveling right into the heart of the storm.

The voice had said something about the moon being directly overhead at the old lighthouse. Gurion wondered if the pull of gravity from the moon had some kind of intensifying effect on the storm. He could see Karyn stroking the arched neck of Lunar Tides, trying to calm him. A week ago Karyn had told the story of how he got the nickname Shooter—something about his quickness in turns and how he shot over the jumps in competition. But today, Lunar Tides seemed a much more appropriate name.

Karyn approached him. "The trail down the north slope

is steeper and more dangerous. Just give Athena her head and she will find her way. Try not to lose me in the fog. But if you do, Athena knows the way. She has been down the trail before and she won't lose our scent."

Gurion nodded and then looked down the trail and toward the storm. Lightning was shooting horizontally across the sky and gathering itself in strange formations that Gurion had never witnessed before. He looked at Lunar Tides, pawing the ground with his one white foreleg. The force of will that pulled Gurion and Karyn toward the storm must have been incomprehensible to these magnificent creatures. Still, against every instinct, they had pushed forward through the fog.

We should get moving again, Gurion thought to himself. I don't know how much time we have, and we have to get to the lighthouse before the break in the storm.

Karyn led them down the narrow path as carefully and quickly as she could. About halfway down they encountered heavy pockets of fog. While in these pockets, Gurion lost sight of Karyn and Lunar Tides, but in the clearings he found them again. Athena followed the trail even when it was invisible to Gurion. Without her, he would have been hopelessly lost.

Once, toward the bottom of the hill, the trail seemed to turn off to the left. Karyn was out of sight for an especially long time, and he was getting a little nervous about finding her again. He urged Athena to the left through the dense fog, but Athena refused to move in that direction.

Lightning struck close to them and Athena reared,

sending Gurion tumbling to the ground. He managed to keep his grip on the reins, and after he had gotten his breath back he led Athena sternly down the path to the left. Within a few steps, the trail ended at a sheer cliff.

Gurion backed carefully away from the cliff, mounted Athena again, and let her have her head. That was the last time he doubted Athena's judgment.

At the bottom of the hill Gurion found Karyn waiting for him at the old road to North Point. Relieved that the worst of the storm seemed to be behind them now, they increased their pace. North Point remained some distance ahead, but the old road, although torn up in a few places, lay flat and straight before them. The horses seemed happy to be running away from the storm instead of heading into it, and they responded with fresh energy.

After twenty minutes or so, Karyn again slowed and finally brought them to a halt. She dismounted, loosened the girth on Shooter a notch or two, and left him to graze at the end of a short tether. Gurion did not need to be coaxed off Athena. They had covered a lot of ground in a hurry, and it felt good to get his land legs again.

After Athena was tended to, Gurion asked, "How much farther to the old lighthouse?"

Karyn checked for landmarks. It had been awhile since she had ridden this way. "At the pace we've been going, I would guess it is a little less than fifteen minutes." She looked up at the sky. "And with the storm behind us and the sun coming out—"

Gurion shot a glance toward the sky and then rushed

for the horses before Karyn could finish.

"It's the break in the storm!" he shouted.

Before Karyn could reach Shooter, Gurion had tightened Athena's cinch and was racing down the road at a full gallop. He knew the way to North Point now and had only one thought in his mind: He must reach the old lighthouse before the break in the storm ended.

Athena sensed his urgency and ran as she had never run before. Gurion kept checking the sky, and as they neared the turnoff to the lighthouse he could see that the clouds were beginning to gather again. Athena stepped gracefully down the narrow walkway that led to the abandoned building and stopped. She had taken Gurion as far as she could. Now it was up to him.

Gurion leaped from Athena's back and ran for the staircase that circled around the outside of the lighthouse. He took the steps two at a time, so when he had reached the top he was completely out of breath. He tried the door, but it was locked. He wanted to scream. He didn't have time for this. The sun was already in danger of being covered by clouds.

He checked the molding over the door. No key. He searched for any kind of likely hiding place, but to no avail. He got down on his hands and knees and checked under the doorsill. Finally, he slipped his fingers under the last step before the landing and found it.

By the time he had opened the door he could see Karyn below. He stepped inside and asked for guidance to find the ring. An old desk and chair occupied the center of the room.

Gurion sat in the chair and opened the only drawer in the desk. There were just two items in the drawer: a Bible and the ring.

The ring had a magnificent crystal setting on a large gold base carved with phases of the moon. Gurion knelt and said words of thanks. He prayed that there would still be time to complete his task and that he would not fail. Then he slipped the huge ring on his index finger and went back outside.

The sun shone brightly between a circle of clouds.

Gurion hurried up the small ladder that led to the roof of the lighthouse. He pulled himself onto the roof and stood in the gusty winds facing the sun. He raised his arms to the heavens and searched for any hint of the moon in the afternoon sky. He could just make out the faint sliver of a crescent directly overhead.

He turned the ring to try to catch the rays of the sun in its glassy prism before the sun was obscured by the clouds. Finally, a beam of light began to form. It shot right out of the top of the ring and headed straight for the moon. Gurion did everything he could to hold the ring steady against the force of the wind, trying to keep the beam focused on the moon. The beam grew stronger and stronger.

After a few seconds, blinding splashes of white light shot out from the ring like a beacon. From where Karyn stood, it looked as if someone had illuminated the old lighthouse, abandoned since before her birth.

In the middle of the beacon she could see Gurion standing, his face to the sun. Before she could call to him, the light broke into a wondrous rainbow that seemed to protect the entire sky. Gurion turned his face toward her and smiled. Then he shimmered, faded, and was gone.

Small service is true service while it lasts:
   Of humblest friends, bright creature! scorn not one:
The daisy, by the shadow that it casts,
   Protects the lingering dewdrop from the sun.
      —*William Wordsworth (1770-1850),*
      "To a Child, written in her album" (1834)

10
THE CHARGE

Gurion felt himself falling. He thought at first that he had lost his balance and tumbled off the top of the lighthouse. But when he tried to look down, he could see nothing—nothing but the white light that had exploded from the ring.

He tried to remember if the lighthouse was on a peninsula. Perhaps he would be lucky enough to land in the water. But surely he would have splashed down by now.

Maybe he was not falling after all. Had his vertigo returned? The flash of light could have disoriented him and made him dizzy. Or he might have been struck by lightning. Yes, the lightning from the storm! Lightning always sought out the highest point, and he had been standing on the top of the lighthouse. Until he fell.

What was happening? Blinded by the white light,

Gurion felt himself falling through space and time. Then the light faded and left him afloat in a sea of transparency.

Gurion's heart began to flutter. His hands trembled. Something must have gone dreadfully wrong. He felt as if he were adrift in an orbit of nothingness, as if he were exiled in the sphere of the forgotten. As far as he could see, he saw nothing. And it seemed he could see forever.

Cold sweat dripped from his brow. He tasted the metallic taste of panic in his cotton-dry mouth.

In an instant of terror, he imagined himself alone, utterly alone, for all eternity. Desolate images of deserted islands, of isolation, began to float menacingly by his window on the world. At first he drew back in horror, repulsed by the ghostly translucence of the images and threatened by what they seemed to forewarn.

But somewhere in the midst of his fear, a realization dawned. As horrible as these images were, they were at least images. The invisible *nothing* that had threatened to overwhelm him had been banished. He had company now, grisly though it might be.

Broken mirrors floated around him, reflecting images of past and future. Gurion could see himself reflected in the fragments. His bearded face seemed to taunt him, like the reflection from the lake. Then the image faded and Gurion could see himself no more. All he could see reflected in the mirrors was the blinding glare of the sun. He turned his head and tried to close his eyes, close out the light, but it was everywhere. An eternity passed, and the images in the mirrors returned. Gurion looked once more for his reflection, but it had changed. The man had become, again, the boy.

Gurion considered the world he had left behind. A dream? Perhaps. But if so, then dreams were as real as any other part of life. Gurion reached out to explore his space. As his fingers felt the bark of the hollow tree, the cobwebs began to clear from his mind. He remembered Kendra's promise that all would be revealed, that he and Dorothy would be privy to all the tree had witnessed over the centuries. Had he stepped from the tree? Who could say what was real and what was illusion?

As Gurion began to accept his situation, his anxiety diminished. He watched the images come and go with interest instead of fear. What began as a slow trickle of pattern and illumination became a virtual parade of images. Some illustrated doubts and fears; some portrayed hopes and dreams. But the majority were examples of service in action.

These examples of service came in a variety of ghostly apparitions. At first the models of service presented to him were grand and almost superhuman. There were images of martyrs dying for their faith, of saints devoting lives to the highest principles, of women and men making sacrifices beyond belief.

Had Gurion's experience with the storm been nothing more than a vivid model of this kind of service for him to ponder? He thought about his own pledge to serve the voice. Would this kind of noble commitment be required?

But not all the pictures that floated before him were of lofty and exalted forms of service. Some were pictures of a service humble and unassuming. He saw a little girl wrap an injured puppy in a towel and hold it lovingly against her body until its owner could be found. He saw a boy give words of encouragement to a frightened classmate. He witnessed an endless procession of these images—ordinary people of all shapes and sizes who bore the unmistakable stamp of caring.

And suddenly he understood.

Serving the voice was not some high calling that demanded supreme sacrifices. No one was asking him to live a perfect life. He didn't have to be a saint or a martyr. He didn't have to devote his life to the church. He wasn't expected to save the world. A finale of images bombarded him like fireworks in a summer sky.

The images flickered and dimmed. He found himself seated in a large chair. His eyes were adjusting to the dark. On a wall opposite him, a lighted chart caught his attention. There were symbols on the chart in neat rows and columns.

"Tell me now, can you read the first line?" a voice was asking.

Gurion squinted and tried to make out the letters, but they were symbols he did not understand.

"No," he heard himself answering. But it was not the answer he really meant to give. He could see the symbols, all right. It was just that he couldn't read them. They were strange to him, some kind of foreign alphabet.

Gurion heard a machine groan, and the symbols on the chart were doubled in size.

"How about now?"

Confused, Gurion looked long and hard at the symbols on the chart. They were like nothing he had ever seen before.

"No." Again, it wasn't the answer he wanted to give. He did not seem to be in control of what he was saying. But he recognized his own voice.

Once again the machine groaned, and this time the symbols were enlarged to ten times their size.

"Can you read them now?" the voice asked hopefully.

The symbols of the first line filled the entire wall. They shouted their message at him. He could see it, hear it, feel it. But he still could not understand it.

"No." His confession was painful. Tears filled his eyes. He could see the letters and the words they formed. Of course he could see them. It was just that he couldn't understand them. That was the problem. No matter how big they were, he still could not understand them.

The light that projected the symbols was clicked off, and Gurion sat in darkness.

"We're going to try a different lens," the voice announced. "It's a simple matter, really. Just a different lens."

From out of nowhere, an appendage of the large chair in which he was seated swung before Gurion's eyes. He heard the machine groan and click through several lenses before the lighted chart reappeared.

"Can you read it now?"

The lens was strong, and the symbols were slightly

blurred. It strained Gurion's eyes a bit to get them to focus. But when his eyes had adjusted, he looked at the symbols and saw the most marvelous sight.

It was as if he were seeing for the first time. Everything was changed. He saw beauty in the world as he had never seen it before. And wonder. All the things he had taken for granted jumped out at him now with an added dimension.

What kind of lens was this?

He looked again and saw beyond beauty and wonder. In the midst of it all, he saw need. But it was not need as he had ever known it before. No, this need perched on the edge of every flower; it peeked out from the heart of every beautiful soul. It was not the kind of need that could be ministered to through a tired sense of duty and then dismissed. It was a need that ran as deep as life itself. In this need, Gurion felt connected to all of life. Every human being was brother and sister to him. Every plant and animal was his cousin.

But through this wonderful new lens, Gurion could see beyond even the measure of need. Beyond the need that ran so deep in the world, Gurion saw purpose—a purpose that blessed his life and filled it with joy.

"Can you read it now?" the voice asked again.

"Yes!" Gurion's eyes blurred with tears of gratitude. "Yes, I can finally read it. Thank you, thank you so much."

"Do you know what kind of lens this is?" the voice asked.

Gurion forced himself to think back over everything he had learned. What kind of lens? Should he know the answer to this question? Finally, he shook his head and admitted that he didn't know.

"It is the lens of love. You are seeing for the first time through your heart."

Again the world around him began to shimmer and fade. And this time he found himself in a large room, standing before an empty gold throne. Gurion approached the throne respectfully, but with a sense of curiosity.

"I keep it as a memento of times long past." It was a voice he knew, the voice that had called him. "There was a time when it was just about the only way people knew how to relate to me. How do you relate to me, Gurion?"

Gurion swallowed hard, then tried to speak. "I . . . I don't really know."

"An honest reply. You can't imagine how refreshing it is to get an honest answer once in a while instead of the usual hypocritical drivel. Do you know why you are here?"

"Yes. I think so," Gurion answered.

"Tell me what you think."

"You are going to tell me what my purpose is, what you want me to do when I get back to my world."

There was a long silence while Gurion awaited a reply, but there was none. Finally Gurion spoke.

"I have seen a vision of purpose."

"Yes?"

Gurion continued. "It was a vision of love and sharing. I felt connected, related to every other living thing."

"And?"

"Well, it sounds stupid, but my purpose was just to be there—to be there when I was needed. And to be available to that need."

"Why does that sound stupid, Gurion?"

"It was as if the only thing that really counted was the needing. As if all the other parts of a person's life had no real meaning without it. I don't know quite how to explain it, but it was almost as if all of life were connected, somehow, through need."

"Gurion, do you understand the meaning of the words chiseled on the wall of the anteroom to the Hall of Service: *Ministrare est vivere?*"

"Dorothy told me what they mean," Gurion answered. "To serve is to live."

"There is life in needing, Gurion. To serve well, you must know how to live, for that is your calling."

"I have been called to serve you. I have taken a pledge to serve you, Dorothy's pledge."

"Dorothy's pledge is not only about serving. It is about living. If you know how to live, you don't have to memorize any pledges. Serving is a consequence of living. I didn't call you just to serve, Gurion. I called you to live."

"To live?"

"Yes, it is by living your life fully that you relate to me, that I can relate to you."

"But every person that is alive is living. I mean—"

"I know what you mean, but it is not so. Being alive is not the same thing as living."

There was a pause while Gurion considered what the voice had said. "I'm afraid I don't understand."

"People who live only for themselves are alive. They eat, they breathe, they work, they play. But they have not accepted the gift of life. The gift of life is a package, Gurion."

"A package?"

"Yes. Every life is interwoven into the fabric of all creation. If you accept the gift of life, you accept a certain measure of responsibility for the world. Life is something we share—we all share together."

For the first time, Gurion felt as if he were putting the pieces of the puzzle together. "That's why needing is so important. We share life through our need."

"And that is why you must understand one more thing before I send you back." A long silence quieted Gurion's excitement and made him ready to listen to what was to follow. "What I need from you is commitment."

"A greater commitment than the pledge?" Gurion asked.

"You will think of the pledge at those times in your life when it seems especially important to serve. But in calling you to life, I am asking of you a greater measure of devotion, a higher dedication, than merely serving when it seems important."

"What kind of commitment do you want from me?"

"I want you to live every day, every minute of every day, participating in the joy and the wonder of the life you share. I want you to take every relationship seriously, no matter how humble. If you would serve me, love the life that I have created. Care for my world in every way you can."

Gurion felt the sun on his face. He could smell the ultraviolet scent of his own sunburnt skin. A fly buzzed around his ear and then lighted on his lower lip. He slapped it away.

His mind was full of cobwebs. His throat felt like cotton from breathing through his mouth. He swallowed and felt his tongue stick to the back of his throat.

He didn't want to open his eyes. He didn't want the dream to end. The log bench felt like a rock beneath him. He was stiff and sore. He must have been sleeping as soundly as the dead.

His head was resting on something soft and lumpy. He tried to focus his thoughts. What kind of pillow was it? His backpack!

The dream. He wanted to try to remember it before it was too late. If he opened his eyes, if he got up and started thinking about something else, he knew he would forget it. He was not very good at remembering dreams. But this dream he wanted to remember.

The island was no dream. He had come to the island to spend his Saturday—or at least that was what he had told his mother. His mother didn't like the island. There were too many stories about it. She had allowed him to come because he was fourteen now, and maybe she knew he would have come even without her permission.

But the voice was the real reason he had come—that inner voice which haunted him, challenged him.

He remembered paddling across the lake through the morning mist. He remembered walking the trail that led to the interior of the island. That was all real. He knew he had not dreamed the island.

After he had walked the trail and sat on the bench, after *that* he was not sure. How much of what had happened after he sat on the bench was real? He didn't know. He didn't remember lying down. But he was lying down now. He must have decided to lie down. He must have fallen asleep.

Was it all a dream?

There was so much to remember. The big spider—no, it was not a spider. It was a man, a man in a black-hooded tunic who moved through the thorny brush like a spider. Did he dream that?

And Kendra? He could still hear the song she was humming.

And Dorothy?

Slowly it all came back to him. The Hall of Service. The doors that led to a thousand other times and places. Wilfred's world. And Cara's. The keeper of the mist. His own nightmare of power. The tournament in the enchanted arena. The hollow tree. The old lighthouse. He could hardly wait to tell Karyn about the storm and the horses and the lighthouse.

He remembered some ancient words that had been chiseled into stone: MINISTRARE EST VIVERE. And the pledge. He remembered the pledge on the scroll of gold.

Then, with a flash of insight, he remembered the voice's final bidding: "If you would serve me, love the life that I have created. Care for my world in every way you can."

Only then did he open his eyes.

Gurion rose slowly from the bench. He glanced at the sun and saw it was still high in the sky. He estimated it was one or two o'clock at the latest. He rummaged through his backpack and found the other half of a peanut butter sandwich.

It had been an incredible dream. He decided that when he got home he would write down every detail that he could remember.

As he ate his sandwich, he stared out across the empty arena filled with sawdust and sand. A cold chill shook his body. And suddenly he wanted to be off this island.

He shouldered his pack and turned to go, but something slowed his steps. There was a deep magic here that he wanted to hang on to. He walked out into the arena and knelt. Unconsciously, he grabbed a handful of sand and let it sift slowly through his fingers.

The sand, the arena . . . they were symbols for the elusiveness of everything that had happened here. Somehow, like the sand and the arena itself, Gurion's adventures were all slipping away into the realm of dreams.

On an impulse, he filled his empty sandwich bag with sand from the enchanted arena and stowed it safely away in his backpack.

One last long look with his heart, and he knew his time here was finished. But he had found enough wonder and enchantment to fill a lifetime.

About the Author

Gary Brewer owns and operates a small used-book store in Talent, Oregon. He and Linda, his wife and love of twenty-eight years, live a charmingly simple life in their home nestled in the foothills of southern Oregon. One young visitor reminisced about a stay with the Brewers, "Mom, I like it here. You can throw rocks in the river and watch the trains go by."

Gary got his theological training at San Francisco Theological Seminary, San Francisco, California. He and Linda have two grown children—David and Carolyn. David plays jazz saxophone and makes his living telling computers what to do. Carolyn sculpts, skis, and is pursuing a computer/art major at the National Technical Institute for the Deaf.